PRETENDING TO BE THE MOUNTAIN MAN'S WIFE

BROTHERS OF SAPPHIRE RANCH
BOOK SIX

MISTY M. BELLER

Cover design by Evelyne Labelle at Carpe Librum Book Design: www.carpelibrumbookdesign.com

ISBN-13 Trade Paperback: 978-1-954810-95-2

ISBN-13 Large Print Paperback: 978-1-954810-96-9

ISBN-13 Casebound Hardback: 978-1-954810-97-6

Where can I go from Your Spirit?
Or where can I flee from Your presence?

If I ascend into heaven, You are there;
If I make my bed in hell, behold, You are there.

If I take the wings of the morning,
And dwell in the uttermost parts of the sea,

Even there Your hand shall lead me,
And Your right hand shall hold me.

Psalm 139:7-10 (NKJV)

CHAPTER 1

October, 1870
Canvas Creek, Montana Territory

*J*ess McPharland stood amidst the rows of dry goods filling the general store, eyeing the shelves stocked with sewing supplies. She'd already located the list of medicines she needed, along with food and a few other items. Now for fabric. She and her father both needed a few more winter clothes.

Father didn't allow her to come to Canvas Creek often, mostly because he didn't want to be bothered with accompanying her. If only he would let her leave the area around their caves without chaperones—or *guards*, one might say. He said it was for protection, but she knew better.

Today, Father and Jedidiah had come with her.

She scanned the room until she found the small, wiry man standing near the far wall. Deep creases lined his weathered face, and his dark eyes missed nothing. Even though he watched from across the space, the weight of his gaze followed everywhere she went. Always ready. That was why Father trusted him so much.

He ranked as second-in-command for all of Mick McPharland's operations. If Father had any dirty business going on, Jedidiah could be found in the middle of it. And if there was honest work to be done, he might be found there too.

For now, though, she could pretend she was free. Free to shop and enjoy herself without worrying about what Jedidiah thought of her. Maybe she could even forget for a little while that she wasn't her own person.

She would always be Mick McPharland's daughter, and he'd never let her escape his control.

He didn't know about the baby yet. As far as she could tell, no one did. She'd known for a little more than two months now, and she had to get away before anyone found out.

She had to find a way to escape.

Freedom. From Father, from this place, from…from all of it.

A voice on the other side of a rack pulled her attention, and she strained to listen without turning.

Jedidiah would come over if he thought she was talking to someone.

"I saw you put that in your pocket." The man's words were firm but not angry.

She couldn't see him or whoever he spoke to, but a young boy's voice squeaked an answer. "I didn't."

Did this man think the lad intended to steal?

Jess moved closer to the end of the shelf so she could step around if needed. If the man worked for the store, he might reprimand the lad, and who knew how far he'd take things. Maybe she could intervene before the punishment got out of hand.

"Are you sure?" The man's tone stayed calm. "I saw something go into your pocket. If it did, we need to take care of it right now."

His tone never rose in anger, nor dipped into that steel-laced rage Father sometimes used.

Most men would have grabbed the boy and yelled or hit him.

Another pause stretched, then the boy mumbled, "I'll put it back."

"That's not what I meant." The man sounded like he was trying to hold back a smile. "I want you to take it up to the counter and tell Mr. Smith what you were going to do with it. Then apologize and promise him you won't ever do it again."

This wasn't the store owner. Did he work there? Whoever he was, he was a different sort of man than she was used to. Kind but firm, even in the face of poor behavior.

A rustling followed his words. "Here." The man's voice held out the last word as if he were offering something.

Jess had to see who this stranger was. She peeked around the end of the shelf, but only saw the back of the man holding out a nickel.

The lad's wide eyes stared at the coin. "You're gonna buy it for me?"

The man nodded. "Only if you mean it when you tell the owner you'll never steal again."

Relief washed over the boy's face. "Yes, sir, I will." He took the money and trotted to the front of the store.

Jess ducked behind the rack before anyone could see her watching them.

As the boy spoke with the clerk, her mind spun. Who was this man? She'd never heard anyone talk to a child like that, let alone one who'd been caught stealing. He wasn't going to punish him?

Boot thuds sounded from around the corner, fading quickly. The man must have stepped away.

She moved back to the bolts of fabric. Father would come to pay for her selections soon, and she had to be finished.

The stranger's voice carried over the barrels between them

as he spoke to the storekeeper. "I'll take another bag of flour too, if you have it."

As she pulled out a roll of blue plaid, she glanced at the man. He looked younger than she'd expected. Broad shoulders filled out his flannel shirt, and his wavy hair was cut shorter than most men wore it.

Maybe he felt her eyes on him because he turned, and their gazes locked for an instant before he dipped his chin and looked away.

He turned to the wall beside the counter where several posters had been tacked up. Wanted signs, most of them. Probably put up by lawmen looking for criminals. And a few job postings.

"Any sign of your brother?" Mr. Smith's question pulled the stranger's attention back.

"I was going to ask you the same." Those broad shoulders slumped a little.

The storekeeper leaned against the counter and crossed his arms. "Sorry. I haven't seen him come through here. I asked Wally to watch for him too. You want me to leave the sign up?"

The stranger dipped a nod. "If you don't mind."

After Mr. Smith handed the man his change and they made arrangements to pick up the goods, the fellow strode out into the blustery fall day.

She carried the blue plaid to the stack of other supplies she'd selected. This would be enough for today. She wanted a look at that sign.

To see it, she had to move closer to Jedidiah, which meant he might start asking questions, but she could evade him well enough. She'd certainly had plenty of practice.

At the wall of notices, she was pretty sure she could tell which one the men had spoken of. The paper was newer than the others, not yet yellowed or faded. And not posted by a lawman with a reward listed. On this flyer, the sketch of a face took up most of the page, a name lettered across the top.

Sampson Coulter

Underneath, only a short message:

> *Twenty years of age, brown hair, able miner.*
> *Family seeking to locate.*
> *Reward for information leading to location.*

Her insides stirred as the name slowly unwrapped recognition within her. Could it be the same Coulter? She'd never heard the man's given name.

Those eyes were unmistakable. So was the shape of the jawline.

Coulter. One of the newer men working in her father's mine.

He must be the brother of the stranger who just left this store.

She had to work to keep from spinning toward the door. Did she dare go after him to tell him she knew his brother? Would Jedidiah allow it if she asked to? Probably not. Perhaps if she went to speak to a woman or child, but not a man. And she didn't dare risk Jedidiah's anger.

She eased out a breath, long and slow so the drop of her shoulders wouldn't be noticed from behind. If she searched for the stranger, she would only put them both in trouble. Maybe she could get him a message through Mr. Smith. Maybe even a note. But what could she tell him? That Sampson Coulter's brother should come out to the most remote mountain around and search until he found a cave? That his brother worked somewhere within?

That would be a disaster for both Coulters. And she couldn't bring herself to put any man at the mercy of her father—especially one who'd just showed such kindness to a child.

~

*J*ess smoothed the patchwork quilt atop her narrow cot, her fingers lingering on the frayed edges. She should stitch a new coverlet soon. Not today though. Father said he would be gone most of the day for some kind of meeting, and sunlight filtered through the cave's mouth, beckoning her outside.

She strode to the opening and adjusted the belt on her split riding skirt as she stepped from their cave dwelling. She was rarely allowed to actually ride in this skirt, but she could move more freely as she explored the mountainside. She'd braided her waist-length hair down her back, and she wore her usual shirt-waist and boots. Not exactly ladylike attire, but practical for life in this mountain wilderness.

The crisp breeze almost made her turn back for a coat, but with the sun so bright, she could manage. If she got too cold, she could always run to warm herself. Maybe a bit of exertion would release the tension that had her insides knotted.

Her hand drifted to the slight bump of her belly. Would jostling hurt the baby?

As she maneuvered the narrow path up the slope, weaving around pines and cedars, her boots crunched against the rocky terrain. The fresh mountain air filled her lungs, and for a moment, she could almost forget the weight of her troubles. Almost.

She paused at a small outcropping to stare out over the sprawling wilderness below. Somewhere in the distance, a hawk cried out, its piercing call echoing through the valley. She closed her eyes, letting the sound wash over her. If only she could sprout wings and fly away. But Father's reach was long, his web of informants and enforcers spread far and wide. Even if she managed to slip away, how long before they tracked her down again, dragging her back to this cage?

The thought made her stomach churn. She couldn't let herself be shackled to Stuart Wallace, the man Father had said he'd force her to marry—another man as controlling as her own father, who saw her as nothing more than a pawn in his games of power.

She sank to her knees on the rocky ground and sat back on her heels, staring up into the heavens. "Please, God." Her voice broke through the peace around her, but speaking aloud seemed to make the prayer more real. "I need help. I need a way out of this darkness. Show me how I can get away for good."

The wind had shifted to a gentle breeze, and the sun's warmth lifted the chill completely.

She considered pretending to want to work in the business. If she did, would Father allow her to move to Fort Benton to act as a shipping agent? The time she and Mama had gone there on holiday had been wonderful. They'd been free to shop and visit the bakery and peruse every store in town. That was one of her favorite memories with Mama.

But Father wouldn't allow it. He hated for Jess to go anywhere near the mine, and he never spoke of his work. He allowed her to tend injuries and sickness among his men— most of the time. He surely wouldn't let her join him in the business. Not that she wanted to have any part in his schemes. Freedom wouldn't be worth the guilt she'd feel every day she helped him.

Sorry, Lord, for even thinking of that idea.

If she went along with his plan to marry her to Mr. Wallace, could she run away from him? No. Her father would send Jedidiah and his men after her. Even as Mrs. Wallace, Jess would still be under her father's thumb. Her husband's too.

A shiver slid through her, and a knot coiled in her middle.

She had to avoid the marriage.

But how?

She closed her eyes, keeping her face to the sun. "Lord, I

need You. I don't know what to do. Send the right person to help me get away."

She let herself linger like that, soaking in the peacefulness. The warmth on her skin.

She didn't hear an answer from God, but this quiet content- edness felt a little like the Lord wrapping his arms around her. If only she could stay cradled in them, relishing this moment always.

The sound of horse hooves clicking against rock drifted from below, and she opened her eyes. Had Father returned already? This was far from his usual route home, so he must have come looking for her. She pushed to her feet and waited, hands clasped in front of her. She'd done nothing wrong, and he wouldn't begrudge her this short walk since she'd already set the house in order.

But the thought of seeing him made her insides tighten, maybe because of the secret she kept from him.

The horse and rider rounded the bend, and her breath caught. Not her father.

The man from the store—Coulter.

CHAPTER 2

*T*he Coulter brother sat tall in the saddle, his shoulders just as broad and his face just as handsome as Jess remembered. When he caught sight of her, his eyes widened, and he reined his mount in.

Her body froze as her mind scrambled to make sense of his presence here. Had he come to find her? She'd just been praying for help. Was this man God's answer?

Of course not. He'd come to find his brother. Had he learned Sampson worked in these mountains? She forced herself to breathe. She'd wanted to tell him herself, so she should be grateful he'd discovered it.

Yet…could his appearing here, a quarter hour's walk past the mountain where Sampson worked as a miner, be God's answer to her prayers?

Maybe.

This man had already shown he would take a stand for right, even when it was hard. Would he help her convince her father to let her go? He'd have to be careful, or he'd find himself with a sound beating. Could he be respectful but not allow her father to push him around?

He still stared at her, perhaps having as much trouble accounting for her presence here as she was his. Their gazes had met in the store, but did he remember her?

She stepped forward, her heart pounding as she raised a hand in greeting. "Hello." Her voice trembled.

He tugged off his hat. "Sorry. Didn't expect to see anyone out here."

She couldn't help a small smile at his reaction. He was so honest and forthright. No hint of secret intentions or cunning. A far cry from the men she'd been surrounded with her entire life.

He looked like he was trying to decide what to say next.

She kept her expression pleasant. "Your name is Coulter, right?"

His brows shot up, and he swept his gaze around the area.

She pressed her lips to keep her smile contained. "You're the brother of Sampson Coulter?"

He straightened, every part of him going alert. "Do you know my brother?" He nudged his horse forward, and the animal picked its way up the path to her.

She waited until he reined the animal to a stop in front of her and dismounted, expectation marking his features. "You know Sampson?"

She dipped her chin. "I do." Was she really going through with this? She had to. God had given her the perfect opportunity to plan her escape. She had to grasp hold of it.

She summoned a fresh dose of courage. "I can take you to him, but first, I need a favor."

~

*G*il Coulter still struggled to catch up with what was happening. He'd been riding along, the same as he had for the last three hours since leaving Canvas Creek. Then this woman had appeared up the slope like a mountain angel.

But this angel knew Sampson. Maybe she really had been sent from above to lead him to his brother. He'd certainly prayed enough for God's help.

"What do you need?"

She gave a tiny shake of her head, then glanced around. A flicker of fear flashed in her eyes. "Come back to my house, and I'll tell you. It's too much to say standing out here." She motioned the direction he'd just come from. "It's only a quarter hour's walk that way."

He'd seen no houses. No barns. Not even animal tracks. But she had to have come from somewhere, and if he'd missed a sign along the way, he'd like to know what it was.

He gave a nod. "All right then. Lead the way."

She started down the slope he'd just ridden up, her long stride moving easily over the rocky terrain. Like a mountain goat, with the grace of a woman in a ballroom and a fancy dress. Probably. He'd never actually seen a ballroom. He and his family had moved from Kansas to the Montana Territory when he was eight. But he could imagine what his brothers' wives had described a time or two.

As the woman ahead of him wove through a patch of trees, he had to scramble to keep up, his horse trailing behind.

He guessed she'd never been in a ballroom either. She moved like she was part of these mountains. Like she'd traveled this exact stretch so many times that she knew every stick and stone.

At last, the path flattened and the trees faded away. He lengthened his stride to walk beside her. "We didn't have a proper introduction back there. I'm Gil Coulter. And you are...?"

She spared him a side glance without slowing. "Jess McPharland."

"Jess. That's pretty." As pretty as she was. "Is it short for something?" As soon as the question slipped out, its impertinence snagged him. He shouldn't be calling her by her given name anyway, much less nosing into its origins.

"Jessamine. Is Gil short for something?"

He grinned. What was fair for one was certainly fair for the other. And he didn't mind giving details. "Gilead. Gilead Jeremiah Coulter."

This time her look lasted a second longer, like she was taking his measure. "That's a mouthful."

"Yep. My three older brothers all have names that start with the letter J, but Mum said she was always calling the wrong name, so she put my J name in the middle."

As a boy, he'd always felt like the outsider because he wasn't in the J clan. But Mum's explanation made sense. She'd certainly called the wrong name enough. Between the six boys and Lucy, she'd struggled. At one point, she'd started calling the boys by number. He'd been "Four." One of the many.

Miss McPharland spoke so little, maybe she thought it odd he'd volunteered that story about his name. But giving details about himself might put her at ease enough to talk more.

Finally, she angled toward a sheer rock face and slowed to a stop. "We're here. My home is just inside."

He scanned the solid stone, but then she moved to the right and disappeared through an entrance he'd thought was just a shadow.

He led his horse to a sturdy scrub bush and tethered the reins, then followed her. A dark cloth hung over the opening he'd thought was only a shadow. Now that he was close, he could see light filtering on either side of the door curtain. And was that the scent of food?

He reached behind his back to check the revolver tucked in his waistband. He likely wouldn't need it, but he'd rather be prepared, just in case Miss McPharland wasn't the only one inside. Surely, she didn't live here alone.

He stepped in, peering around the cloth until he could see what lay within.

As the scene opened before him, he blinked. Was this a mirage?

Such a cozy home. It could have been the inside of a log cabin if not for the stone walls. Lanterns lit the space, and a cookstove sat to his right against the outside wall, a pipe protruding through the stone. He'd not seen smoke rising outside. It must have been hidden.

A trestle table sat in the middle with four chairs tucked around it. On his left, long curtains hung from the top of the cavern to the floor, probably to create a sleeping space. For how many?

He turned to the woman, who stood at the stove, ladling something steaming into a wooden bowl. "This is a nice home."

"We call it our apartment." She focused on her work as she spoke. "Are you hungry? I've had soup simmering, and it should be ready." She sent a cheery smile his direction as she carried the dish to the table.

In here, she didn't even seem like the same woman he'd walked with outside. Or rather, practically run to keep up with. Now, she looked as domestic as one of his sisters-in-law, serving up a meal to a hungry brood of Coulters after a long day's work with the animals or in the mine.

This version was just as lovely as the mountain angel he'd first seen. She wore her hair in a long braid that swung as she shifted, adding grace to her fluid movements.

She set the steaming food on the table, then returned to the stove to pour a dark liquid into a wooden mug. Steam rose from the cup, and the aroma of coffee made his middle pinch as if he'd not eaten all day.

When she turned to take the drink to the table, she gave him another expectant look, motioning to the chair in front of the food. "Come sit, please. I'm sorry if I surprised you outside. I was just a little...taken aback to see you there."

He huffed a breath. Taken aback for certain. He *still* hadn't fully regained his senses.

He stepped to the table but stood behind the chair. "Are you going to eat too?" He wouldn't be sitting until she did.

She slipped into the chair across from him. "I'm not hungry."

Should he protest? Maybe best to just start this conversation so he could figure out what she needed and get her to take him to Sampson. He pulled out his chair and eased into it nowhere near as gracefully as she had.

The seat was sturdy, though, and he let his weight settle against the back.

Jess folded her hands on the table, her gaze finally meeting his. "I need your help to escape my father."

Gil stared at her. This woman was nothing but surprises. Escape? He glanced around. A hat hanging on a peg in the wall was the only sign of a man.

He leaned forward, bracing his arms on the table. "Your father?"

She nodded, her expression clouding. "He's...a powerful man. Controlling. He doesn't let me leave the caves without a guard." She seemed to realize she'd been outside moments before when they met. "I can go for walks in the area, but not far. Never to town by myself, and I'm not allowed to speak to anyone. He and a guard watch me, one always keeping an eye on me."

Gil could see where she might feel like a prisoner in need of escape. He'd felt that way every now and then himself, back before Jericho eased his fears of strangers coming onto their ranch. That had taken some time and a few hard conversations, but Jericho had finally relented—thanks to a lot of work from God and the threat of losing Dinah, the woman who was now Jericho's wife.

Gil kept his voice calm and reasonable. Maybe he could help start that same work here. "Why can't you just leave?"

Pain flashed across her face. "I've tried. A few months ago, I made it all the way to Helena. But Father's men found me and brought me back." A smirk marred her beautiful face. "He's powerful, my father. And he has spies everywhere. The only way I'll ever be free is with his blessing. And the only way I can imagine receiving that..." She took a deep breath, as if steadying herself. "Is if he believes I'm married, and thus, beyond his control."

She waited, and he tried to sort through what she might be saying. He wasn't usually so dense, but this entire situation had his brain slogging through fog.

Then a flash of understanding slipped in, and he jerked back from the table. "You want me to marry you?"

Her eyes widened a little. "No, of course not." But the uncertainty in her gaze made it seem like she'd thought about saying that very thing.

Her shoulders lifted as she inhaled. "Just pretend. Pretend to be my husband."

CHAPTER 3

*G*il could only stare at the woman. *Pretend.* Not actually marry her. But still...

"Just for a few days." Her voice was pleading. "Long enough to convince my father. Then I'll take you to Sampson, and we can all leave, together."

It was a crazy plan. Dangerous, probably. What kind of man must her father be to drive her to such desperation? Or was she addled? Maybe her father was really kind, doing his best to care for her. Maybe she didn't have a father at all.

He eased out a breath. "How do I know you're speaking the truth?" A question from earlier slipped back in. "And how do you know who I am and about my brother?"

She dipped her chin, acknowledging the fairness of his questions. "I saw you at the general store last week. In Canvas Creek. You caught that boy stealing and made him admit what he'd done to the clerk."

Once more, he raised his brows at her. His mouth was hanging open, too, so he shut it. "How could you know that?" He'd made sure to stay out of sight when the lad approached the clerk with a somber face and the nickel.

The corners of her mouth tugged, and a smile lit her eyes.

His pulse responded, surging until his chest tightened. She was... *Beautiful* didn't begin to cover it. An angel. She had to be. How else could she take his breath with only a tiny smile?

She opened her mouth to speak, and he leaned in so he didn't miss a word. "I was in the next row over. I'm sorry I listened in. I suppose I should have made my presence known." The smile faded from her eyes, taking with it all the light. "My father had a guard watching me. He wouldn't have let me speak to you."

Gil strained to remember who else had been in the store. He'd spent enough time in town these past few weeks, searching for Sampson, that he'd recognized most of the faces in the store that day. He'd even recognized the lad from passing him in the streets a time or two.

But there had been one man near the door... A bit on the small side, he didn't look strong enough to be anyone's guard. He wore his years in the deep lines of his leathery face, just like all the older miners in the area did. Gil'd had no reason to suspect he was anyone else than a miner come to town for supplies, lingering in the warmth the store's woodstove offered before he headed back to one of the dilapidated shanties down by the river.

Gil honed his gaze on Miss McPharland. "What did the man look like?"

She frowned. "Jedidiah? He's short and wiry. Doesn't look like he'd be much trouble, but he's brutal. And his men are loyal. They won't cross him. They know better."

That first bit described the man he'd seen. The latter...well, Gil had been shielded from men like that since they moved to the Territory. But he still remembered the Montgomery's gang who rode through Fort Scott, where they'd lived in Kansas. *Brutal* described them. Men who wouldn't blink an eye before they'd shoot a woman or child at point blank range. Like they didn't own a conscience. Or a soul.

Miss McPharland was watching him, her gaze unreadable. If her father was associated with men like that, she did need to escape.

And she'd said she could take him Sampson. They'd been searching for him over a month now. If he could just find his brother, he could convince him he'd be welcome at home.

If finding Sampson and protecting this woman required him to get into her father's good graces by pretending to be her husband, he could do that. He'd always had a gift for settling tense situations. A few pleasant words, a little something to make people smile, and they forgot about their anger or worry enough to think rationally.

Before he could commit to her plan though, he had a few more questions. "What makes you think your father would believe our ruse? I've never met him. If he never lets you leave here, how could we be married?"

Something flashed in her eyes—embarrassment maybe?— but then her face sobered. "Remember I said I tried to run away a couple months ago?"

He nodded.

"I was gone for three days before they found me." She shrugged. "Enough time for a ceremony."

He could imagine how she would answer his next question, but he had to ask it anyway, just to tease her. "I've generally thought it would take me more than three days to get to know a woman before I proposed marriage." Though it had taken him less than an hour to decided he would agree to her proposal now.

For a *fake* marriage. That was the difference. No matter how a part of him wanted to suggest the real thing.

A ridiculous part of him, obviously.

Like he'd just said, he'd need to know the woman a lot better than he did this one before he'd contemplate spending the rest of his life with her.

She wrinkled her nose. "I plan to tell him we met when I was picking berries. You were riding through the mountains looking for your brother. You've been in the area a while, and we continued meeting." Again, she shrugged. "It's certainly founded on the truth, just not the same timing."

He let silence settle as he mulled through the other things they'd need to consider.

She waited quietly. So many people couldn't be so patient, always needing to fill the noise or rush off to get things done.

After another minute, he leveled a look at her. "If your father is the kind of man you describe, how will he react to the news?"

Her mouth pinched. "He has...other plans for me—a match that's advantageous for him. He won't like it."

The news shot down Gil's spine. "You're betrothed?" Another surprise shouldn't shock him. But truly, what other shocking news would she casually share?

"I've only met my so-called intended once. He's twice my age. While he was crossing the street to meet us at the cafe, he kicked a dog and then backhand a boy who was trying to get out of his way on the boardwalk." She narrowed her gaze. "During the conversation, he ate his food as well as half of mine while boasting about how powerful he was in whatever mining town he came from. His exact words were, 'There's not a man for miles around who isn't under my thumb. Some come easily, others learn the hard way.'"

The way she'd lowered her voice to a man's pitch might have been humorous, if not for the desperation in her gaze. Her eyes pleaded with him even more than her words did. "I don't know if he'll be worse than my father, but he's the same kind of man. I can't risk it."

Gil would be tarred and feathered before he let her be legally bound to a man like that. But there was one more question he needed to ask, now while she might be most open to answering. "Where is my brother?"

She pulled back a little, her gaze searching him. Was she looking for something in particular? Or trying to decide whether to answer?

He leaned forward, letting her see his earnestness. "I'll help you, Miss McPharland. But I need to know that you really can take me to Sampson. I've been searching for him for weeks now. If he's in this area, I have to find him."

She regarded him a few more seconds. "He works for my father. He's done so for more than a month now. When we've convinced my father we're truly married and feel confident he'll let us leave together, I'll take you to your brother."

The way she pressed her mouth closed made it clear that was all he'd get on the matter. It was enough though. The daughter of a man like she described may not be entirely trustworthy—after all, she was asking Gil to help her deceive her own father—but he'd get her to safety, whether he received anything in return or not. But if he could possibly find Sampson and the sapphires stolen from them at the same time, he wouldn't let the opportunity slip through his fingers.

"I'll do it." He extended his hand across the table.

Her eyes grew wide. Because of his nearness, or did she not know that was usually part of business dealings?

Whatever the reason, the way she looked so startled would never do.

"Jess." He kept his voice gentle and used her given name, as he would if they were married.

"Yes?" She blinked, her voice weak.

He had to bite back a smile. "If we're husband and wife, you'll have to let me touch you. There's no way we can convince anyone if you shrink back from my hand."

Fear crossed her features, making itself evident in the trembling at the corners of her lips. What had he said?

You'll have to let me touch you.

He was a clumsy, numb-brained oaf.

He leaned back and gripped the edge of the table on his side. "I didn't mean it like that. Not *touch you*. Just...touch you." He raised his hand, palm up. "You know. Like your hand."

He was making a mess of this. Where were all his charming words when he needed them? He had to get them past this, and maybe he could even pull a smile from her in the process.

He hunched low to be eye level with her. "I'm sorry, Jess. I said that all wrong. But it makes me realize there's something that needs to be said between us." He swallowed to moisten his throat. He needed her to hear this clearly. "I'm honored that you asked for my help. Honestly, it scares me a little to think what might have happened if you asked someone you couldn't be sure would value a lady's..." The heat searing his neck wouldn't quite let him get the word *virtue* out. So he pushed on.

"I promise I won't misuse your trust. We will have to be friendly enough to be convincing, but I promise I won't touch you in any way that's indecent." He let out a breath. Surely she understood the point he was trying to make without him having to turn any redder.

He half-expected her to have that little smile at her mouth at his embarrassment, but instead, her eyes held a sheen of moisture. Had he made such a mess of it? Or was she so affected by his promise to be honorable?

By the openness in her expression—was that wonder?—his insides twisted. She must have only been exposed to men with the lowest of characters in this remote place.

Sampson was working with these men?

That thought knotted even tighter in his gut. Had he become like them? Surely not. His brother was young and ambitious, no doubt, but he'd been raised just like the rest of them. He wouldn't turn his back on God and decency completely.

Would he?

Gil had to find him, soon. Had to get his little brother away from this place. And now Jess too. He'd doubled his mission, but he would fulfill it. He had to.

CHAPTER 4

*J*ess pulled the pie from the oven and set it atop the cookstove. Was it underdone? That would be better than burnt even a little. Father hated burnt food. But if the dried apples weren't soft enough, the pie she'd baked to put him in good spirits would have the opposite effect. She poked the knife tip into the apple that peeked through the opening in the top crust. Soft enough.

She slid it onto the warming burner, then turned to see what else could be done. Her gaze tugged her all the way around to the man sitting at the table.

Lands, he was handsome. The way one corner of his mouth tugged upward, revealing a dimple. Those rich brown eyes, the slight wave in his brown hair.

He was watching her, as he had been every other time she'd looked back at him. She should be accustomed to it by now, but her nerves were tangling tighter and tighter with every quarter hour.

She almost wanted her father to come in now, though time without him was usually precious.

She and Gil had taken his horse to the pasture where

Father's other mounts grazed, then they'd spent the rest of the afternoon preparing for their conversation with him. Working through details about when they'd supposedly married and how long they'd been courting before that. They both agreed he shouldn't give her father his real surname. Father knowing the connection between Gil and Sampson could only make the situation harder. Gil had chosen his mother's surname before she married—Standish.

As they'd talked, Gil asked a few personal questions, too, like whether she liked to read and what books she preferred. Turned out that, like her, he loved *Gulliver's Travels*. And they'd shared stories from their pasts so they could answer with some truth should Father ask them questions about each other.

It was hard to fathom Gil's large family and how close-knit they seemed, evidenced by the warmth in his eyes as he'd spoken of each. The three older brothers had already taken wives and built their own cabins on the family ranch. He'd lost his older sister and both parents, just as she'd lost her mother. Was it easier to lose someone special when you had plenty of people around to share the grief? Maybe that didn't matter. Jess couldn't imagine not missing Mama, even all these years later, no matter how many people had mourned with her.

But Gil had been very lucky—or rather, blessed—to grow up surrounded by so many people who loved him. How would that feel? It didn't seem possible. She had no experience that could help her imagine.

A tiny yearning pressed in her chest as she returned her focus to the stove. Did she dare ask him to take her to his family's ranch? Did they allow outsiders to live there? Of course not. It was a *family* ranch, not a common town.

Jess would have to find her own way. Build a new life using whatever she could get from selling her mother's jewelry. She'd have to find work quickly, perhaps as a housekeeper or a cook.

If she could satisfy her demanding father, she should be able to please any employer willing to pay her.

The whisper of leather on stone outside made her heart lurch, yanking her out of her thoughts. Father was back. She glanced at Gil, then moved toward him.

He rose from his chair and met her partway.

As her father stepped into the room, she inhaled a breath and sent up a silent prayer. *Lord, protect us.*

The moment Father's gaze struck Gil, he halted. His gaze narrowed, never leaving the man beside her. "Who's this?" His voice took on a roughness he used with his men but almost never with her.

She took a small step forward and forced out the words she'd rehearsed. "Father, I have news for you. I hope you'll find it good news." She found Gil's arm beside her, wrapping her fingers around the thick cord of muscle. She'd not expected so much strength, but she used the contact to draw strength of her own. "I'd like you to meet my husband, Gilead Standish."

Her father's gaze swung to her, his eyes dark. "Husband?"

She fought to keep from shrinking back. "Yes." Should she volunteer more information? Or wait till he asked?

His gaze shifted back to Gil, and he worked his jaw as though chewing on his words. His face turned even redder than Gil's had when he'd made the promise not to take advantage.

At least Father was trying to stay calm, though he hated surprises, and he especially hated when his plans were thwarted. Maybe she should have eased him into the idea of this. It wouldn't have worked though. Confronting him was the only way to convince him she told the truth.

At last, he spoke again, still using that rough voice. "Stop playing games. Who is this man?" He still stared at Gil, his eyes flinging blades, but the words were clearly for her.

She forced herself to speak with a steady tone despite the fear pulsing in her heart. The more calm she showed, the better chance Gil would be too. "I'm being earnest, Father. This is my husband, Gil. We've known each other for several months. When I went to Helena in August, we were married."

She took a slow breath, then let it out just as slowly.

Father wouldn't attack Gil, would he? His gaze had turned so dark that she couldn't be certain anymore.

She inched sideways, a little in front of her *husband*. "I wasn't sure how you'd react or how best to tell you, so we kept our marriage secret until now." She gave the look that usually melted her father. "But I couldn't wait any longer. I know you'll love him. He's such a good man."

Gilead moved around her and stuck out his hand toward her father. "I'm glad to finally meet you, Mr. McPharland."

But Father didn't take his hand. His gaze never left Gilead's face, and he made no move to return the greeting or speak any words.

At last, he moved his focus back to her. Was he shaking? When he spoke, his voice was as solid as the stone walls around them. "I'll have it annulled. Or you can pretend this farce never happened. Wallace need never know."

Farce.

Did he suspect they were lying? Her pulse galloped impossibly fast. He'd not meant it that way though. Just that it wasn't acceptable because it wasn't what he'd planned.

It didn't benefit him in any way.

But what if Father tried to force her to marry Stuart Wallace against her will? There was no real law in this area to stop him. Only one thing would make him change his mind. He'd have to know Wallace would never take her if he knew the truth.

Which meant she had to tell him the truth—or part of it, anyway.

Her breath caught in her throat, nearly strangling her. She had to say this.

Lord, help me.

She swallowed and hoped her voice wouldn't shake. "There's something else you should know too." She reached for Gil's arm once more, needing to appear happy about this, though her forced smile must've wobbled. "I've just recently realized I'm in the family way. We're going to be parents." She sent Gil a strangled smile, doing her best to ignore his rounding eyes, before turning back to her father. "And you'll be a grandfather."

The room fell silent.

Father's face turned ashen, his eyes widening in shock before narrowing into slits of anger.

Gil didn't move, his arm tense under her grip.

"You're what?" Her father's voice was a low growl, each word sharp as a knife. "Carrying this man's child?"

Jess swallowed hard, her throat tight. She held on Gil's arm as if he could shield her. "Yes, Father. Gil and I...we're married, and we're going to have a baby." She tried to keep her tone even, but her voice quavered.

Her father's gaze flicked between them, and his mouth formed a hard line. When he finally spoke, his eyes locked on her, his voice deadly calm. "You've really done it now, girl."

Jess flinched at the fury in his tone. She'd seen him angry before, but she'd never had his rage directed at her. Fear coiled in her belly, but she forced herself to stand firm. For her child's sake, she had to be strong.

Once again, Gil inched in front of her, shielding part of her with his body. "We hoped you'd be happy, sir. We sure are." His voice held such a genial tone that she could almost believe he really was her husband, that they'd been overjoyed to learn of their coming babe.

A bit of relief eased the knots in her shoulders. Gil was here, helping her. Playing his part better than she could have hoped.

Her father's icy stare locked onto him. "I don't even know you, boy. What's your name?"

"Gilead Standish, sir. My family owns a ranch southwest of here."

Something in her father's expression shifted. That frightening anger never left his eyes, and his jaw stayed hard as steel. Even so, something was different. She couldn't name it, but it was there. She'd spent a lifetime learning her father's moods, the shifts in his face, his voice. What she saw now, the change in his expression—the mystery of it, the not understanding... It terrified her.

"What are you doing in these parts, Standish?" His voice was even, yet still laced with fury.

She slid a look at Gil, praying he wouldn't tell her father the truth about his purpose here. Father wouldn't hesitate to hurt Sampson to get to Gil if he learned their connection.

Icy dread slipped through her, freezing her chest. She tightened her grip on Gil's arm.

Gil cleared his throat. "Exploring. Enjoying a bit of time away from the ranch. Also keeping my eye out for an uncle. He and his family came to these parts before we did. Now that my parents have passed, my brothers and I would like to find him."

She eased out a breath. He was smart.

"You've nice land around here," Gil said. "Good valley land for grazing. Do you keep any cattle?"

He was making conversation. She had to work to keep the shock from her expression. Here they were, trying to keep her father from venting his rage, and he was making small talk.

Studying Gil, another unreadable look filled her father's eyes. Calculating maybe? Surely, he was trying to figure out how he could work the situation to his own good. He dipped his chin in a nod. "I suppose so, but we don't run cattle. That's what you raise on your...ranch?" Why had Father paused before that last word?

"Yes, sir. My father started with horses when we first moved to the place, and we added cattle about five years ago."

Her father seemed to choose his words carefully. "That sounds like a lot of work. I'm surprised your family could spare you so long." His gaze slipped to her, leaving his meaning clear.

Gil's voice didn't shift from its casual tone. "I've several brothers and a nephew still working the ranch." He glanced at her, his free hand touching her fingers still wrapped around his arm. The smile that touched his mouth lit in his eyes with a tenderness that felt so real, her heart gave a little flutter. "I'm eager to take Jess to meet them. They'll love her."

Gil turned back to her father. "I hope you don't mind us traveling for a bit. We haven't made any final decisions about where we'll live, but I want her to meet my family."

Her father just glared, and everything inside her clenched as she watched for the anger to take over once more. But it didn't. His tight skin eased into what looked dangerously close to a smile. "I suppose that's fair. We can talk more about it later." He stepped forward, and she fought to keep from flinching. But Father extended his hand to Gil. "Welcome to the family, son."

Gil didn't pause before taking his own step and meeting the grasp. "Thank you, sir."

Just like that?

But as she exhaled, unease twisted in her gut.

That had been too easy. Her father never gave in so readily, especially when his plans were thwarted. What was he plotting behind that suddenly friendly demeanor?

As if sensing her disquiet, Gil released her father's hand and rested his fingers back on hers, still gripping his arm. She didn't dare release him, the only thing holding her steady.

Glancing up at him, she found him watching her with those warm brown eyes. *Trust me,* they seemed to say. *We'll get through this together.*

Drawing strength from his steady presence, Jess lifted her chin and met her father's gaze. "Thank you, Father. Your blessing means everything to us."

"Yes, well..." Her father waved a dismissive hand. "What's done is done. No use crying over spilt milk, as they say." His gaze sharpened on her. "But Jess girl, you know how I feel about secrets between us."

A chill skated down her spine. "I know. I'm sorry for not telling you sooner. I just...I needed to be sure..." She faltered, unsure how to finish.

Once more he waved the words away. "I need to speak with Jedidiah, so hold my dinner till later." He started for the door, but paused and turned back to Gil. "I look forward to knowing you better, son." Without waiting for an answer, he strode out.

CHAPTER 5

a heavy silence settled in Father's wake. Jess's knees trembled, and as Gil turned to her, realized she must look awful.

His brows drew together, and he gripped her elbows, holding her upright. "Let's sit down." He half-guided, half-carried her to her chair at the table.

She had to push past this weakness. Her father hadn't hurt Gil. Hadn't even tried to. She should be relieved. Maybe that's what this was—relief. Yet why was panic welling in her chest so thick she could barely breathe?

Gil pulled his chair around the corner of the table so he could sit beside her. His thigh pressed against her skirts, but the contact felt secure. Steady. Everything about Gil made her feel secure.

He propped his elbows on the table and leaned in. It seemed like he didn't know what to do with his hands, but then he closed his palm over her hand. His grip was solid, the calluses on his skin only adding to the feeling of security. This man worked an honest job for a living. He wasn't manipulative and scheming like her father.

Father's hands had always been smooth yet hard. Father was as different from Gil as the darkness of the cave from noontime sunshine.

She let herself meet Gil's eyes. Let herself soak in their warmth. Let her body relax, streaming out the tension with her spent air.

He was waiting for her to speak. No hint of hurry in the air between them. She had to find a way to thank him. Words wouldn't begin to voice everything inside her, but she could start there.

"Thank you, Gil." Her voice cracked on the second word as emotion surged through her. Why was she having so much trouble controlling her body these days?

An easy smile met his eyes, crinkling the corners. "I'm glad I could help. I don't think it went so bad either."

She could only gape at him. "Were you part of the same conversation I was?"

That twinkle in his eyes was enough to throw any girl off-kilter. "Sure. He'll settled in to the idea. I think we'll become good friends, he and I."

She nearly choked on the breath she sucked in, which kept her from saying her first response. He must be jesting. His smile meant he was teasing surely. If he knew her father, he wouldn't joke about the situation.

Then his expression sobered. "Anyway. Could I see my brother now?"

She glanced toward the door curtain. They still had several hours left in the day, but she didn't dare take Gil through the passageways where they were most likely to be seen by her father. Not yet.

She returned her focus to her new *husband*. I don't think it's safe to take you to Sampson yet. We'll talk to him tomorrow. After my father has had time to adjust to...things. We can see him from a distance though. There's an old tunnel that's not used anymore where we'll be able to look down on the cavern where Sampson's working."

She pushed to her feet and started toward the wall where she hung her wrap.

"Jess, wait." Gil sounded more serious than she'd heard him yet. Enough to give her pause.

She turned to face him.

Gil had followed and now stood far closer than she'd expected. She had to tip her chin up to meet his gaze.

Confusion marked his expression, and maybe a bit of wariness. "What does my brother do here?"

She should probably tell him everything. They'd come too far to withhold details now. And he'd more than accomplished what she'd hoped with her father. "Sampson works for my father. In the mine."

Gil's brow gathered even more. "For your father? What did you say his name was?"

The weight in her chest threatened to cut off her breathing. "Simon McPharland. Most people know him as Mick."

Gil's expression shifted from confusion to worry to…something else.

She took a step back.

He didn't look angry. It was the recognition she saw. How did Gil know her father? Must've been by name only, for neither had seemed to recognize the other.

Father's name was known widely. She knew this.

But how did *Gil* know him?

She'd thought he was different, not associated with any of the lowlifes her father mingled with. Could Gil only know of him through his more reputable endeavors?

No. The clarity in Gil's eyes, the way his mind seemed to be putting pieces together, the way he now looked at *her*…

Did he learn about her father because of his search for Sampson?

If only she knew how and why Sampson had come to be here. She didn't usually want to know those details, didn't want to be part of her father's false dealings. She could do nothing to stop him, and knowledge of his actions would only infuriate her —and maybe make her do or say something she would regret.

So she kept her focus on caring for the men when they were hurt or injured. Sampson had experienced neither, so she only knew him in passing.

Gil straightened, then motioned to the door curtain. "Let's go then."

Something in his manner was different now. He still wore a pleasant expression, but it seemed more focused, as if he had a plan he intended to act on.

Did she dare take him down to the mine? What if he did something that made himself stand out. What if he tried to sneak away with his brother?

She couldn't let him leave without her.

She softened her voice. "Maybe it's best you stay here. I'm not going all the way into the mine. I should be able to watch the men from a distance. If there's something amiss with your brother, I'll see it and let you know.. It will be harder to stay quiet if there are two of us. I'll take you to talk to your brother tomorrow."

The lines around Gil's eyes softened. It must have been determination she'd not been able to identify a moment ago, but it eased now. "I won't make a scene, Jess. I promise. I just... well, I didn't realize your father was Mick. Sampson mentioned him once, and I figured I'd find my brother some-where around him." He shrugged in an almost self-deprecating way. "I guess I did. I won't cause trouble. I won't take a step unless you tell me to. But I've looked a long time for my brother. It'd mean a lot if I could just lay eyes on him, see for myself he's all right."

She searched for any hint of duplicity, any sign he might be trying to wheedle into her good graces. He looked sincere, he'd proved discerning when he'd spoken to her father.

"All right." She hoped she wouldn't regret this. "But stay with me. And be quiet." She didn't know for certain Father would be angry if he caught her bringing her *husband* into the mine, but she'd rather not learn for sure.

~

*G*il followed Jess out of the cave, slipping around the cloth door and out into the sunshine. She'd brought a lantern, but it certainly wasn't needed out here.

She must be planning to go into another cave.

As before, he had to lengthen his stride to keep up with her quick step. She'd clearly traveled this path many times.

And it *was* a path, but not one he'd have ever found if not for her. She led him around the base of the mountain that contained her cave home. The tall grass on one side concealed the trampled dirt they now walked.

He kept his voice low. "Is this the way your father went?" If so, they might meet him coming back. Would the man expect them to have stayed in the house?

"No, he would have taken the inside cave."

Inside cave?

She veered left, behind a cluster of cedar trees no taller than he was. He had to turn sideways to follow, with the cliff wall at his back and branches scratching his face and hands.

A narrow cave opening soon became clear beside him. How many hidden entrances into the mountain were there? And how long had she and her father lived here? It didn't seem possible they could have kept the openings and paths so hidden for years, but Jess maneuvered them like she'd done so all her life.

She lifted her lantern as they stepped into the darkness. "Stay close and be quiet." She spoke just above a whisper, still not glancing back to make sure he was there. Maybe she wanted to lose him. More likely, she could hear his noisy footsteps. No matter how he tried, he couldn't keep his boots as quiet as hers, especially not now, with all the loose gravel littering the stone floor.

He tried several different ways to land his feet and finally settled into the one that made the least noise. It helped that this stretch didn't have much gravel.

Jess stopped abruptly and set the lantern down. She turned to him, her face half in shadow. "We go on without the light. You have to stay quiet."

The importance of that last statement hung between them. With the lantern casting odd long shadows over her face, he couldn't read anything in her expression except seriousness.

What did she fear?

Too late to ask now.

She crept forward, and he stayed close. As they left the lantern behind, darkness pressed in, heavy and blinding.

He reached out to make sure he wouldn't run into anything. In this thick black, he couldn't be certain whether he was about to slam into a rock wall or a jutting stone. His toe kicked a loose stone, sending it clattering against the wall. Like a gunshot in the stillness.

"Shh!" Jess hissed so low, it almost sounded like a breath.

The noise didn't come from ahead of him though. More to the right. Perhaps he had been about to walk into a wall.

"Take my hand." Her words might have been only a thought.

But then her fingers brushed his wrist. He slid his hand until her palm fit against his.

She started forward, nearly dragging him the first step until he caught up. When this woman set her mind to do a thing, she wasted no time.

He settled into the same stride as her, walking just behind but not so much that he would step on her heels. In the murky darkness, her hand provided something solid to focus on. Her skin was soft at first contact, but when he concentrated, he could feel a slight roughness on her palms and fingertips. She was no stranger to hard work, like most women who made their home in the west. But Jess's life seemed so different than those of his sisters-in-law that he wouldn't have been surprised if her skin were pale as milk or soft as honey.

Reality was far better though. She was the perfect blend of feminine grace and competence.

She was so small, her hand nearly engulfed by his. Yet her grip possessed a wiry strength, much like the woman herself. He didn't have to hide his grin in the darkness. Jess McPharland was like no other woman. Thank the Lord he'd come upon her. What if she'd asked another man to play her pretend husband?

His chest tightened at the thought of someone else holding her hand in the darkness. Some cad eager to take advantage of her.

Or even a decent man, come to think of it.

This was *his* place.

Which made no sense whatsoever, except the *rightness* of it sank deep inside him. He might have stumbled into far more than he'd expected today, but he couldn't be sorry he'd met Jess.

He nearly chuckled, remembering when they'd spoken to her father. She must have decided she wouldn't be able to convince him of the truth of her marriage, so she'd added that bit about being in the family way. Jess was sharp, no doubt about it.

Thankfully, he'd have her far away from these caves before her falsehood became clear. No telling what her bully of a father would do or say if he learned she'd lied about all of it.

Jess led him around a corner.

Wherever she went, he would go too. Who knew what threat might loom in this darkness. She was so small. That feeling welled up in his chest again—that overpowering need to protect her, to shield her from any danger or threat. No matter what the cost.

It was irrational to feel so deeply about a woman he'd just met, but there it was, as solid as the stone all around him.

If he'd doubted her story, her father's behavior proved all she'd told him. She'd lived under her father's thumb and was desperate to get away, certainly to escape before being forced to marry a man she didn't love.

Gil couldn't let any harm come to her. Especially here, in this suffocating darkness where peril might lurk.

A steady pounding rose from up ahead. He realized he'd been hearing it, but now the rhythm was loud enough to distinguish from his own heartbeat.

Metal striking metal. Or maybe stone. The sound grew louder as they advanced.

A faint light appeared ahead, and Jess's pace slowed. Her grip on his hand tightened. Was she nervous?

Just ahead, the rock wall on either side fell away, and the ground changed to a wooden bridge spanning a deep chasm. Jess slowed just before the bridge. She inched to the place where the railing met the rock and peered down.

Gil had to rise up on his toes to see over her head.

About fifty feet below, five men struck the rock wall with pickaxes. It only took a moment to find Sampson, his wiry frame unmistakable even at this distance.

His brother swung the pickax three more times before a chunk of stone broke free. He dropped to his knees and ran his hands over the rock, his movements eager, almost desperate, as if he were mining his own sapphires rather than toiling for Mick MacFarland.

Gil's heart clenched.

What kind of hold did Mick have over Sampson to make him toil away in this godforsaken pit? What poisonous promises had the man fed Gil's little brother to keep him enslaved here, scrabbling in the dirt for another man's treasure?

Gil tightened his grip on the railing until the rough wood bit into his palms. Somehow, he had to get through to Sampson, to free him from Mick's clutches before something happened to his brother. The question was, how?

And he had to find a way without endangering Jess in the process.

His throat itched to signal Sampson—to whistle the sound they used on the ranch—something to let him know his big brother was here now. That he wasn't alone.

But he'd promised Jess he'd stay hidden and silent. He eased back so he could try to read her expression in the dim light. Her brow was furrowed as she watched the men below, her lips pressed into a thin line.

She met his gaze with gathered brows, maybe worried he'd do exactly as he wanted to do, exactly what he'd promised *not* to do.

He offered a single nod. He wouldn't betray her.

He turned his attention back to Sampson, who was now using a hammer and a smaller pick to chip away at the stone he'd separated. His brother's movements were practiced, efficient, evidence of all the years he'd helped in their own mine. Sampson preferred to work with the animals, but they'd all spent long days cutting out the sapphires.

After a few more minutes, Jess tugged on his hand, motioning for them to go back the way they'd come. He backed away, letting her take the lead. He kept her hand as before while his mind spun. He'd come here to find Sampson and bring him home. They could leave tonight if his brother were his only concern.

But he had to recover the sapphires stolen from their mine—an entire wagonload of fully packed crates, worth over two hundred thousand dollars. He couldn't leave without the sapphires, which they'd toiled to gather for an entire year. His brother Jude had worked the hardest. He'd been the most devastated over their loss. Gil couldn't stand the thought of Jude coming after Mick himself. He couldn't lose another brother to this man.

He could simply ask Jess where the sapphires were, but he dismissed that idea just as quickly. She had already risked so much by bringing him here, by agreeing to let him see Sampson tomorrow. Would she answer him truthfully if he asked? He didn't know her well enough to say for sure.

Maybe Sampson knew where the sapphires had been taken. Then the three of them could take back the gemstones and sneak out tomorrow.

He prayed that was the case.

In the meantime, he needed to prepare for Mick's return this evening. Keeping on that man's good side would likely take every ounce of charm and tact Gil possessed, especially knowing now that this man had stolen from Gil's family.

The falsehood about Jess being in the family way made the whole scheme even more complex. That particular lie couldn't hold forever.

But Gil would get her away long before that. Away from the dark caves and her father's iron grip. Every person deserved so much more than this shadowed half-life. And he wanted to be the one to show it to this woman.

The rightness of that desire settled deep in his bones as they finally reached the lantern. In the flickering light, Jess's face was drawn and pale. She started forward again, whispering over her shoulder. "Let's get back before my father returns."

Mick McPharland. From what Gil had learned, the man was as cunning as he was ruthless, and one wrong move could spell disaster—for Gil, for Sampson, and for the woman who walked ahead of him, the woman he'd vowed to protect at any cost.

CHAPTER 6

*G*il stepped into the dimly lit cave-home behind Jess. Her lantern light joined the only other light in the place.

When he'd first entered after meeting Jess, she'd had several lanterns blazing and the place felt cozy. Now with only these two, the stone walls felt like a prison. Confining. How could they live in such darkness all the time?

The savory scent of stewed meat and dumplings filled the air, and Jess moved directly to the cookstove to stir what she'd toiled over so long earlier. His stomach growled in anticipation. He'd only eaten a few hours ago, but maybe all this tension and pretense made him hungrier than usual.

She turned to him with a tired smile. "Have a seat. Dinner's ready."

"Smells good." He moved to the rough-hewn table, easing into the chair he'd used before. He had a direct view of the door curtain from here, so he'd know the moment her father entered.

As he settled in, Jess brought a steaming bowl and mug to the table, placing both in front of him. The rich scents rising from the food made his belly cramp. The soup she'd served him earlier had been good, but this smelled remarkable enough to make him keel over just from breathing in the steam.

He gripped the spoon she'd tucked in the bowl, then looked up to see when she'd be coming with her own portion.

She was wiping the work counter beside the stove, moving with deliberate motions. Not in a hurry at all. Did she not plan to join him for the prayer? He'd not been obvious about it earlier because she'd had so much on her mind, but this felt like the official evening meal.

He cleared his throat. "Aren't you coming?"

She glanced back at him. "I'm not hungry. Too nervous, I suppose." She gave a tight smile.

She had to eat. Everyone did. He was concerned about their situation, too, but skipping meals would only sap his strength. The same for her. It seemed she'd need a bit of coaxing though.

He rose and crossed to the stove before he could second-guess himself. He didn't miss her wide eyes when she turned to watch him, but he kept his focus on his actions. After grabbing a bowl from the stack where she'd gotten his, he lifted the pot lid and dipped the ladle inside to scoop out a few plump dumplings and chunks of deer meat. He only filled the bowl halfway—about how much the women on the ranch ate at a meal—then replaced the cover and turned to her.

She looked like a cornered rabbit.

He offered his best encouraging smile, then stepped closer and reached out to gently slip his arm around her back. She started to pull away, but he kept his hand secure, curving his fingers around her side for a slightly better hold. He wouldn't force her, but he wanted to offer significant encouragement.

"Wife, it would please me greatly if you'd share this meal with me." He smiled down at her face, which was tilted up at him. this close, he could dip his head and kiss those lips. She had a faint dusting of freckles he'd not noticed before, which made her look strangely delicate. A good reminder to tread carefully.

She wasn't stepping forward, even though he'd added a little pressure.

He added a little pleading to his smile. Her shock seemed to ease a little at that. Her mouth pinched, but no anger sparked in her eyes. Maybe she was holding back a smile.

He gave her back another little nudge. "Please?"

Now the corner of her mouth twitched, and she let out a sigh. "All right. I'll sit down with you anyway."

He kept his triumph from showing but didn't let up on his grin as he guided her to the table. "Thank you."

Once he placed the bowl in front of her and helped scoot her chair in, he went back to pour her a mug full of whatever heated in the carafe on the back of the stove. Tea, from the smell of it.

After settling that and a spoon in front of her, he went around to his own seat and pulled in close to the table. He reached his hand across the wooden surface, palm up. "Shall we pray for the meal?"

Her gaze flashed wary, but she took his hand and bowed her head. Maybe he shouldn't push for so much contact between them, but that seemed to be a struggle for her, and if they were going to convince her father that they were not only married but had been intimate enough to produce a child, she needed to get used to his touch. Nothing improper, but she couldn't back away with her eyes as big as plates every time their hands brushed.

The fact that his body surged to life with every contact was a nice extra for him. He worked to center his focus on God. "Lord, thank You. For this food. For Jess and all the ability you've given her. For guiding us to meet just the way we did today." He had no doubt God had led him to her. She needed help. And without her help, he might never have found not only Sampson, but also the very man who'd ordered the theft of their sapphires.

He searched for the right words for his request. "Lord, give us wisdom to know how to proceed. Show us each step. Give us favor with Jess's father, and help us accomplish what we need to here. In the name of Your Son we ask these things. Amen."

Jess didn't immediately jerk her hand from his after that last word, and when he opened his eyes and lifted his head, she was watching him with a sober expression, one that made him think she'd been focused on each word of his prayer. Or maybe even praying her own.

"Thank you." Her voice came soft. Almost reverent.

He nodded, then released her hand, despite the fact that he'd rather keep hold of it through the rest of the meal. And the rest of the night, for that matter.

He took up his spoon and let himself scoop a full bite into his mouth. Sweet mercy, but this was good. So many flavors and warm enough to ease all the way through him as the dumpling practically melted in his mouth.

Jess was watching him, and he gave a smile that hopefully showed his pure pleasure. "Best dumplings I've ever eaten. No doubt about it."

Her cheeks tinged pink, and she dipped her head, focusing on her own food as she scooped a tiny chunk of meat. As much as he loved watching her, his belly needed another bite. Now.

His food was half gone by the time he looked up again.

Jess was staring down at her bowl as she swirled her spoon around the dumplings. It didn't look like a one of them was missing from what he'd ladled out.

"Aren't you going to eat that? It's too good to pass up."

Her smile was weak as she nudged a dumpling on her spoon.

Maybe conversation would help distract her. There were a few things they needed to talk about anyway. He took his own bite, relishing the taste, then swallowed. "I guess we should figure out... I mean, do you have thoughts on tonight?"

She jerked up to search his face, that wariness touching her eyes again.

He cleared his throat. "I mean sleeping. Won't your father expect...?" He didn't have to finish. Her bright red cheeks said she understood his meaning perfectly.

Her eyes cut to the fabric hanging to divide off one corner of the room. "My bed is over there. It's not... I mean...." She darted a glance at him before focusing on her food again. "It's small. Not really big enough for..."

Was it wrong of him to chuckle at her embarrassment? He wasn't laughing at her exactly. She was just so cute when her cheeks flushed like that.

"You can keep the bed. If there's a spot big enough on the floor, I'll be fine with it." Even as the words came out, a niggle of concern slipped in. "Unless... Will your father look behind the curtain? Will it make him suspicious if we're not in bed together?"

She hesitated, finally shaking off her embarrassment as she considered. "The bed really isn't that big. I'm not sure the two could lay side by side without one falling off." Her brows lowered. "He generally doesn't go near my things. I don't know if he'll be different now, but..."

He shrugged. "If there's not room, there's not room." Though he'd sure be amenable to testing that to be certain.

From the looks of her, she wouldn't. And it wouldn't be proper. "It'll make sense for me to be on the floor for the short time we'll be staying here. I hope we'll be able to leave in a day or two."

The line of her shoulders eased, and her brows relaxed. She returned to stirring the gravy around her dumplings. As far as he knew, she'd only taken that single bite. Did he need to prompt her again? The last thing he wanted was to be annoying. Maybe he could try a different tact.

He leaned across the small table and used his spoon to scoop a dumpling from her bowl. Then he lifted it toward her mouth.

She eyed the bite, almost glaring at it.

He raised the spoon to level with her chin. "Have a bite. You'll like it."

She shot him a look, but the amusement was there in her eyes.

He lifted the spoon a little. "Best dumplings I've ever tasted. You don't want to miss them."

The line of her mouth cracked as its corners lifted in a reluctant grin. At last, she leaned forward and closed her mouth over the spoon. She probably didn't mean the bite to be as seductive as it was. She'd blushed when speaking of sleeping arrangements, after all.

But as she closed her lips around the spoon, then pulled back, taking the dumpling with her, she lifted her eyes to his.

Everything in him went still. His mouth dried up. His breath stopped moving. And did his heart stop beating? The only thing in him that continued working were his eyes. And a lot of other parts of him that wanted to push this table aside and pull her close, letting her lips close around his as they had that spoon.

Mercy, this woman got to him. She was beautiful. Breathtaking. Fragile. Strong.

And *not his*.

Only his pretend wife.

A woman who still stiffened at his touch. They'd only met today, so he probably shouldn't expect more. Had it really only been this morning when he'd ridden out of Canvas Creek, trying to maintain a thread of optimism that he might actually find Sampson?

He'd done that and so much more.

Jess still held his gaze as she chewed. Was she trying to set him ablaze? Maybe she couldn't look away either. For sure and certain, even if he wanted to break the connection between them, he couldn't do it. Her eyes were dark and intense, the richest navy he'd ever seen—at least, in this dim lantern light.

She blinked, dipping her focus to her bowl.

Something in his chest cracked. He'd never felt such a need for someone, so intense it brought a physical ache when they weren't connected, either by touch or locked gazes or...

He let out a breath. He needed out of this room. Fresh air. Something, anything to clear his mind. To get his senses back.

He scooped the last of his food in one large bite, chewed twice, then swallowed and stood. "I need to water my horse."

Jess's gaze pressed into him, but he turned away, striding for the only exit from this pressure chamber.

As he stepped out into the cool night, he inhaled a long swig of fresh air, filling up his lungs until they could hold no more. He let it out in a slow stream, releasing the tension of the past hours. He had to keep his wits about him. If he didn't, he might make an error that cost them all far more than he could stand to pay. There was far more at stake here than his heart.

CHAPTER 7

*J*ess stared into the darkness as her other senses took in her surroundings. Her body said it must be morning, though the cave made it impossible to tell for certain. The steady sound of Gil's breathing drifted from the floor beside her. Not snoring, just deep and even.

And so close.

In this tiny, curtained chamber, there was only enough room for her bed, a chair, her dresser, and Gil's long body. If she reached down to the floor beside her bed, she could tap him on the shoulder.

Father's snores from beyond the curtain echoed through the cave, nearly drowning out Gil's breathing. But that was a noise she knew well. All her life, she'd slept and awakened to his snores.

The steady rhythm meant all was as usual.

Except now it lied.

Nothing was as it had been yesterday morning, though she'd awakened to the very same sound.

She slid a hand over her belly. When she stood or sat upright, she could feel the beginning of a swell. But lying on her back like this, she could almost imagine her life hadn't forever changed.

How could she possibly raise a child on her own? Would she be a good mother? She'd have to work, but what would she find that would provide enough income and allow her to be with her babe? Would she be forced to leave her child with someone else while she went to her job? Someone she didn't know? Someone she would be forced to trust?

She couldn't imagine, didn't even want to consider it.

She cradled her hands over her middle. *I'll do my very best for you. I promise. I won't let you grow up in a cave. You'll have sunshine and freedom and love. So much love.*

Tears pricked her eyes, and she closed them to ward away the liquid. A few drops squeezed out anyway, sliding down her cheeks to dampen her hair.

She needed to get up and start her day. Whenever these emotions started to overwhelm her, action was the only way to regain control. And heaven knew she needed as much control over as many aspects of life as she could manage.

As she pushed the covers aside and sat up, she focused on the sounds of Gil's breathing and Father's snoring. Both stayed steady. She'd become a master at rising soundlessly to prepare the morning meal.

Father didn't like unnecessary noises, and she'd learned long ago that the best way to wake him was with the aroma of bacon and hot cakes.

He'd returned late last night, even later than she'd expected. In fact, she and Gil were already preparing to bed down.

Father hadn't been in the mood to talk, just ate quickly and said goodnight. No civilities, but also no anger. How would he be today?

She slipped out of bed, careful not to let the wood or ropes creak. Walking on the stone floor made it much easier to keep quiet.

As always, her first task was to light the wood in the cook-stove's firebox. Since she'd prepared it last night before bed and left the metal door open, now all she had to do was strike a match and light the kindling. Over time, she'd learned how to keep from making noise—no clanging metal or scraping stone. No dropping anything.

She blew out the match and set it on the stove to cool. She'd already filled the carafe with water and coffee grounds, so it could be heating while she stepped outside for her morning ministrations.

Her shawl didn't provide nearly enough protection from the icy dawn air, pushing her to hurry through her ablutions and slip back inside. Steam already rose from the kettle in the faint light drifting through the door curtain. She used a twig from the fire to light a lantern, then focused on preparing batter for the hot cakes.

Father's snores hadn't stopped, so all was well.

After adding milk and oil to the flour, she stirred the batter, careful not to scrape the spoon against the bowl.

A rustling met her ears, and she froze, straining for the source.

Another noise, this time feet shuffling on stone. Since her father still snored, that must be Gil rising. Had she awakened him? She'd been so quiet. Would he be angry like Father any time she accidentally interrupted his sleep?

When he pulled the curtain aside and stepped into the main room, she raised a silencing finger to her lips.

The sight of him, rumpled and sleep-dazed, swept away all coherent thoughts. He'd looked strong and confident yesterday. Now, with his hair sticking up at odd angles and his shirt untucked, he looked so...tender. So familiar. Like she could go to him, wrap her arms around his waist, and rest her head against his chest. Offer a good morning greeting.

Maybe even cup that scruffy jaw in her hands and pull him down for a kiss.

She turned away before those thoughts could take root. Gil wasn't her real husband. He was a stranger. She'd best not let quiet moments like this confuse her.

As she scooped spoonfuls of batter and plopped them in circles in the warm frying pan, Gil ambled toward her. She slid a glance to see if he needed something, but he only looked curious as he watched her work. He stopped at the side of the stove, then simply stood there watching the food.

Once three hot cakes were cooking, she set the bowl back on the counter and laid strips of bacon in her other pan.

Still Gil said nothing.

She looked at him again, brows raised. Did he have questions or need something? She should probably explain their morning routine. But if she whispered even a word, Father might wake. Should she take Gil outside to speak? Or maybe just hand him a cup of coffee and gesture for him to sit at the table.

Coffee. Of course, that was what he wanted.

She poured the dark brew into a mug and handed it to Gil with a small smile.

He took it, then stepped closer to her, coming up right beside her. Before she could move or even think what he might be doing, his hand landed on her back—warm and steady—and he leaned in over her shoulder.

She froze. He was so close. That strong palm warm through her dress, the pressure of his chest against her shoulder. Her hair caught in the scruff on his face. The warmth of his breath brushed across her ear.

"Where can I help?" The words, in the barest whisper, sent a shiver through her. He must have felt it. Her entire body had trembled.

She inhaled to steady herself.

But how could she speak or even think with him this close?

His breath caressed her cheek, and that hand still anchored her to him.

She shook her head, trying not to let the movement pull her away. Not because she wanted to stay here against him—of course not—but just so he wouldn't think she was reacting. Or maybe so he wouldn't notice at all.

He didn't ask more questions though, only held her in place as they watched the hot cakes bubble. His presence felt...overwhelming. Strong yet gentle. The strength of his body seemed to seep into hers, making it impossible for her to move, even if she'd wanted to. And if she turned toward him, those lips would be right there. A breath away

Would he kiss her?

The thought stole everything else. Every unanswered question. Every niggling worry. Even Father's snores faded until all she knew was Gil, beside her, holding her against him. A man who might kiss her if she gave any indication she wanted him to.

A flash of memory slipped in.

Her first kiss with Alex. She couldn't even say why she'd allowed it. Other than the fact that she'd wanted something different from this monotony. Something she could control. Allowing the kiss. Then allowing more. She'd been in control... until she'd allowed herself to believe the fantasy that Alex might be her way of escape. And then her own self-control had slipped.

Her throat ached and her eyes stung. One little mistake now...and it could cost her the freedom she wanted more than anything.

"What is it?" Gil's whisper came just as softly as before, but the weight of his chest against her back eased. He shifted sideways, angling so he could see her face. How had he even known something was wrong?

She blinked to quell the emotion. She shouldn't have let the memory slip in. She certainly wouldn't ever again make the mistakes she'd made with Alex. Not with Gil or anyone else. She simply had to make sure she kept herself under control.

She shook her head to show nothing was wrong, then reached for the mug of coffee he'd put down at some point— though she couldn't have said when—and placed it once more in his hands. With a smile, she pointed to the table, careful not to meet his gaze. He had a way of looking inside that saw too much. And his warm brown eyes drew her in, making her do things she wouldn't normally do.

He didn't move.

She turned back to the stove to flip the hotcakes over, the intensity of his gaze warming her neck. But then, he turned to the table.

As he retreated from the edge of her vision, Father's snore shifted to a grunt. She cringed, in no hurry for him to wake up, then forced herself to relax as the sounds from her father's chamber faded completely. He would come out soon, and she needed to be ready.

A moment later, the curtain rasped open and Father stepped into the main room, his heavy footsteps echoing in the quiet cave.

Jess sent him a smile and called out a soft, "Good morning." He always came out fully dressed, and this time he looked as if he'd brushed his hair too.

Gil's voice also offered a steady, "Good morning."

Father nodded toward her, the only response she'd get, then his gaze swept across the table toward where Gil sat. He slowed to a halt.

The silence stretched, heavy with tension. With Gil directly behind her, she couldn't see him, but she could well imagine the sight that made her father pause. Gil at the table, coffee in hand, while she cooked breakfast. The picture of domesticity. But not the one Father was used to.

He started forward again, and his chair scraped across the floor when he pulled it back to sit. "Smells good in here."

She was already scooping food onto his plate. After adding a fork, she poured his coffee and carried the meal to the table with a smile.

Father sat in his usual place, beside what she'd begun to think of as Gil's chair. As she placed the dishes in front of her father, she met Gil's gaze and tried to signal that she'd bring his next. Father would want the first serving, and there was no use angering him without necessity.

Gil's eyes held a slight twinkle. Whether he understood her expression or not, he didn't seem miffed about being neglected.

Father started in before she brought Gil's plate to the table, and after seeing they both had all they needed, she turned back to keep herself busy at the work counter. She should go refill her bucket of clean water, but she couldn't leave the cabin while Father ate. He'd want her nearby in case he needed something.

"Aren't you going to eat?" Gil's voice broke through her thoughts.

She hesitated, still facing the counter. It was the same question he'd asked last night.

Did he plan to feed her this morning too? Memory of taking the dumpling from his spoon surged through her, flooding her neck with heat. They certainly couldn't recreate that scene in front of her father.

But maybe she could fill a plate and sit with them. Father had never told her *not* to eat with him. She'd just always found it easier to stay on her feet so she could bring what he needed— coffee refills, more bacon, and the like. After he left for his day's work, she could relax and eat alone, without her stomach knotting as she tried to anticipate his needs.

She turned to answer Gil, checking her father's expression first to see what he thought of the question. Father was focused on his food, forking a bite of hotcake. Maybe he wouldn't mind.

She reached for a clean plate and added a hotcake and two strips of bacon. The food didn't look appetizing, but it was what she had always eaten in the morning. Shouldn't she be hungrier since she was eating for two? The babe was so tiny, though, he or she must not need much extra yet.

As she settled into her chair across from Gil, Father took a swig of coffee, then set the mug down with a clunk. "I suppose we need to talk about plans."

Her middle tightened. Would he try to make their plans for them? She slid a glance at Gil before she started to speak.

But he beat her to it, nodding to her father. "We were thinking to stay here another day or two, then head on to my family's ranch."

She held her breath, though she did her best not to let her apprehension show. Would Father allow them to leave freely, or would they have to negotiate?

He finished chewing his bite of hotcake. "That'll give me enough time to finish up a few things. Thought I'd go along with you, meet your folks. See where you plan to settle my daughter." He slid a look at Gil that was clearly meant to make Gil defensive.

Gil didn't step into the snare though. Instead, a tinge of sadness touched his eyes. Was it feigned? "My folks passed a few years back. My brothers are on the ranch still. Four of them."

Father eyed him as he bit into a thick slab of bacon. "I'll meet them then. What say we leave Sunday? That's four days from now."

Gil seemed to consider that before he turned to her. "Does that work for you?"

Her throat went dry. What did he expect her to say? Was he looking for information in her face? Like whether he would get to see his brother by then? Or was he asking whether he should commit to Father's plan? Of course they couldn't let her father accompany them, but they'd have to figure a way out of that later.

She gave a bright smile that she hoped hid her worries. "Perfect."

Father didn't force much conversation after that, just cleaned his plate. After gulping a final swig of coffee, he pushed to his feet. "I'll be in and out today." He strode to the wall beside the door and pulled his hat from the peg as he turned back to them. "What are the two of you doing?"

Jess's heart stuttered. This sudden question felt like a test. What would he want her to do with Gil? Keep him away from the mines, most likely.

She spoke quickly, before Gil could come up with something. "I thought I'd show Gil some of the views from Triangle Mountain. Maybe take him to the little waterfall." Both were places Father let her roam on her own. In fact, Triangle Mountain was where she'd met Gil yesterday.

He nodded. Did his eyes narrow on her? Maybe not. He settled his hat on his head. "I'll be back at noon to eat."

She managed a smile. "I'll have the meal ready."

His expression softened. "Thanks, Junebug."

That old familiar nickname tightened her throat. It'd been a while since he called her that, but it brought back a flood of memories from sweet moments. The times he'd read her a storybook as a child. Took her on walks to the waterfall. Taught her to ride a horse. Mama had been part of some of the memories, but some had been just her and Father. Back then, she'd not questioned whether he loved her.

The reminder of so much happiness together made her almost feel guilty for questioning his love now.

CHAPTER 8

*H*ow many caves could there be, hidden inside this mountain?

Gil followed Jess into the darkness of a new tunnel, this time slipping between two boulders that hid the opening. Her father had been true to his word the night before, arriving late and sitting quietly at the table with his food. They'd all bedded down soon after, with Gil stretching out on a blanket covering the stone floor beside Jess's higher bed. As he lay awake, listening to the sounds of Jess's steady breathing nearby, he'd assumed sleep would be long in coming. But about the time McPharland's deep snores filled the air, exhaustion took over Gil's body too.

This morning, he'd helped with her chores and saw to his gelding, and now she was finally taking him to Sampson.

Jess's lantern lit the tight space. At least the ceiling was higher here than the other tunnel.

She started forward, and he stayed close behind her. This cave was too narrow for them to move side-by-side, but he'd like to remain in the light.

The rough-hewn angles of the stone around them showed this corridor had most likely been cut out by hand.

His family didn't use blasting powder at their own mine, so he hadn't seen much of what an explosion left behind, but the flat angles around him looked more like the cave in their sapphire mine he and his brothers had been cutting out little by little these past few years.

The clamor of pickaxes striking rock sounded in the distance, a hollow ringing that bounced off the stone walls.

This mine appeared to be a massive operation, as deep as these tunnels went into the mountain. Hand-cut as they appeared, it would have taken many men over the course of years to cut so far in.

The passageway opened into a cavern, the lantern's flickering light casting eerie shadows across the jagged walls. This room was smaller than the one she'd brought him to the night before. Three men worked pickaxes against the stone, filling the air with *clangs* and heavy breathing.

A quick glance showed none was his brother. The one on the left was too stocky. In the middle, the fellow appeared too old. Really old, as Gil looked closer, and far too frail. The man on the right was shorter than Sampson and had pale hair.

As she strode through the cavern toward the older man, all three paused in their work. They turned to her with smiles— which faded the moment they saw Gil.

The old fellow kept his focus on Jess when she reached him, but the other two miners returned to their work, the clanging just as overwhelming as before. How could anyone stand this noise? He'd have to ask Jess later how long these men worked in the caverns each day. Surely not long.

Jess leaned in to say something to the man, and Gil halted a few steps back to give them privacy. Not that he could overhear with this racket.

She glanced over her shoulder and motioned Gil forward, slipping her hand around his upper arm when he was close. She leaned up to speak into the old fellow's ear. "Ezekiel, I'd like you to meet my husband. Gil Standish."

The man's gaze had been locked on her mouth, reading her words most likely. But now it flicked up to her eyes, his own narrowing for just a second, as though making certain he'd heard right.

As much as Gil would like to see the expression on Jess's face, he didn't want to miss whatever Ezekiel might communicate with his eyes. The marriage must surprise him.

Ezekiel turned to Gil then, unwrapping gnarled fingers from his pickaxe to extend his hand. "Pleased to meet you, Gil." His voice quavered with age.

Gil grasped it, meeting the man's gaze with a nod. "Same here, sir."

The pickaxes had ceased again, the other miners watching this meeting.

Ezekiel's hand was rough with calluses and dirt but not as strong as Gil would have expected from a fellow who cut through stone every day—even one who had a few years on him. Maybe he hadn't been working here long.

As Ezekiel held Gil's hand a little longer than usual, his eyes regarded him with a depth of wisdom and knowing that seemed to see all the way to his soul. "I'm sure there's quite a story behind this union, one I'd very much like to hear." He gentled the words with a warmth in his eyes and a tugging at the corners of his mouth.

He turned back to Jess, and those brown eyes softened even more. "How are you, Miss Jess?"

She released Gil's arm as though finally relaxing. "I'm all right, but what of you? How's your cough? Have you had any more breathing troubles?" Her brow furrowed as she studied him.

Ezekiel waved off her worries. "The Lord provides me with the breath I need each day. It's plenty enough."

Jess touched his sleeve. "And your shoulder? Is it still paining you? I can come back with liniment to rub on it. I'll be here at the lunch hour when you have a break."

The old man patted her hand. "You are a blessing, sweet lady. But truly, God gives me all I require, another day to sing His praises and do His work."

How could this man have so much joy in the midst of a life in this place?

Jess and the old miner locked gazes, faded eyes meeting sharp vibrant ones, and a wordless conversation passed between them. Jess's face softened, and her lips tugged. A weight appeared to lift from her shoulders. How long had they known each other? Long enough for Jess to trust him...far more than she trusted her father, it seemed.

At last, she turned away and bid farewell to all three men. Gil did the same, and the clamor started up again as he followed her into another tunnel, this one wide enough for them to walk side by side.

When they'd moved away from the noise, he spoke quietly. "Ezekiel seems like a good man. How long has he worked here?"

In the swinging lantern light, her expression was hard to make out, but her voice held a smile." About three years. I've asked him why he stays, why he doesn't go somewhere easier. But he always says the same—the Lord called him to serve in *this* mine, called him to *this* work and to *these* men."

She slid a look at Gil. "I wish he didn't have to work so hard, but I'm thankful he's here. He's the one who taught me about God's grace. My own faith is nothing to his, but I'm learning. Day by day."

Tension eased from Gil's chest. He'd been hoping she knew the Lord. He'd thought so from the way she'd prayed before the meal last night, but this confirmation gave him relief. Even within the depths of this mountain, with a father like hers, God had found a way to reach her. *Thank You, Lord.* The farther they walked, the more the grade sloped downward. The dank scent of moisture grew stronger.

They emerged into a larger cavern. It only took a heartbeat to realize this was the same one Jess had brought him to the night before. Except now they were near the bottom, gazing up at the towering walls and the wooden bridge they'd stood on before.

He scanned the space, taking in the four miners scattered around. His heart pounded as he searched for the familiar face of his brother.

There. Across the cavern.

Sampson was frozen, his pickaxe resting on his shoulder, staring at Gil with wide, disbelieving eyes.

A grin pressed up from Gil's chest, relief and joy surging through him at the closer sight of his brother—alive and whole.

He started forward.

But Jess grabbed his sleeve, jerking him to a halt.

He glanced at her, sending a question in his eyes, but she wasn't looking at him. Instead, her gaze had fixed on two men standing nearby, a false smile plastered on her face as she tugged Gil in their direction.

Every part of him wanted to pull away from her, to go to Sampson at last. But she must have a reason for stopping him.

He walked beside her, studying the two men. Both were familiar, but it took a second to recognize them.

He'd seen the taller man working last night, and the shorter fellow was the man from the general store in Canvas Creek, the one Jess had said had been there to guard her. She'd said his name... Jedidiah?

Wariness gripped Gil's gut, and he prepared for whatever the man might say or do.

Jedidiah watched their approach with hard, calculating eyes, his expression giving nothing away.

They halted close enough to speak, which was easy enough since the men in this cavern had all ceased pounding.

Jess's grip on Gil tightened. "Jedidiah, I don't think you've met my husband, Gil Standish."

The man studied him with a cool, measuring stare. He dipped his chin in a curt nod, but said nothing.

Gil offered an easy smile, something to show he bore this stranger no animosity.

Not yet anyway.

"Good to meet you, Jedidiah." He turned to the other man, the miner, who'd eased back. "And you, sir." Just because the fellow performed grunt work didn't mean he had to be invisible. Besides, since Jedidiah had been speaking with him, this man might be one of those eyes and ears Jess had mentioned were scattered around the area. It would be good to know him.

The miner gave a quick nod. "Howdy." It seemed he didn't plan to share his name.

Better not to push the question now. He needed to appear amiable and unthreatening so he wouldn't raise suspicions that might hinder his real purposes here.

Jess kept her voice bright as she motioned to the far end of the cavern. "We came because I want to show Gil the stalactites over there." She tugged his arm, and he obliged, giving the men a farewell nod.

The cavern stayed quiet as he and Jess strolled across the open space to the shadowed far side. As much as he wanted to speak to her—and look at Sampson—he didn't dare do either.

By the time they reached a section where long calcium icicles hung from the ceiling and rose up from the floor, the murmur of men's voices sounded again from behind them. He couldn't make out any words, which meant he might be safe speaking to Jess quietly. He'd rather not give them the idea that Jess had brought him here for any reason other than seeing the natural wonders.

She motioned to a section where the stalactites grew thicker and clearer. "Those are my favorite." She kept her voice low, still gripping his arm.

He rested his hand atop hers to give what assurance he could.

Gil guessed she hadn't planned to see Jedidiah and would make sure the man didn't cause her any problems. He kept his tone low and natural as he answered her. "It's been a while since I've seen any so clear."

She slid a look at him, curiosity in her gaze. Was she surprised he had experience in caves?

"We have a good friend, Two Stones, who used to take my brothers and me exploring. We scouted out lots of caves and caverns, and saw plenty of strange formations. Not many as pretty as these though."

Her brows gathered. "Two Stones? Is that a nickname?"

He shook his head. "He's Salish. One of the best men I know. Like a brother to us all."

She nodded. "Well then. Shall we go back?" She still used that cheery tone, as if Jedidiah were standing behind them, scrutinizing every word.

They turned and saw that the man was still speaking to the miner, and both were too far away for Gil to pick out any of their words. Either Jess was unusually cautious by nature, or she'd learned to be so from previous experiences. Most likely the latter.

Help me keep her safe, Lord.

They ambled back the way they'd come, her hand tucked around his elbow, his own hand covering hers. Just like a courting couple strolling in a park.

He slid a glance at Sampson without turning his head. His brother had dropped to his knees and was sorting loose stones on the ground. What had this Jedidiah man done to Sampson to make him pretend not to know his own brother? Anger twisted through him as possibilities flooded his mind. Whippings? Threats?

He forced himself to clear away those thoughts. He had to give the appearance of calm. Just an interesting outing with his new wife.

Jedidiah had stopped talking and now watched them approach.

Gil urged Jess to continue past the man. He offered Jedidiah and the other fellow a farewell nod as they stepped into the dark hallway. He slid a final glance at Sampson before the wall hid him.

Sampson was looking from the corner of his eye, though he hadn't stopped riffling through the small stones on the ground. He didn't quite catch his brother's gaze, but at least Sampson had dared to look.

Was he keeping quiet so he didn't get in trouble with Jedidiah, or was he doing it for Gil's protection? Maybe he realized Gil had come into the mine on a ruse and was waiting for Gil to make the first move. That seemed a bit more calculating than Sampson's normal manner, but maybe nearly two months of working for Mick McPharland had taught him to be shrewd.

His gut turned sour. He had to get his brother out of this place before something awful happened. The sapphires too. He'd promised himself he wasn't leaving until he recovered the full load—assuming it was still here and not already sold off.

And Jess. Now he had to get her away too. He would do it. All of it.

CHAPTER 9

*G*il wasn't sorry Jess didn't release him as they walked through the shadowy cave. It felt almost as though she'd forgotten that she held his elbow. He waited until they were nearly back to the smaller cavern, the pounding of pickaxes louder and louder, then leaned in close to talk.

She tightened her grip, and he hesitated. She turned a smile on him he barely caught in the shadows, but her eyes held a bit of a wild look, one that screamed, *Don't speak.*

He pulled back, then gave a little nod. Did she think Jedidiah had followed them? It was possible.

Gil strained to hear the sound of footsteps behind, but the pickaxes drowned out everything except the swish of Jess's skirts. He'd have to be patient and wait to ask his questions when they were away from this place.

They passed through the smaller cavern without stopping, though all the men there acknowledged them with a nod or a smile.

Gil wanted to stop and speak to Ezekiel again, maybe ask about Sampson. Surely the older man knew him. Maybe he'd even taken him under his wing, been a sort of father-figure. Sampson was only twenty, after all.

But Jess didn't even slow her steps, like she was set on a course out of these caves.

He couldn't deny the urge for daylight himself, and away from this deafening racket.

At last, they slipped between the boulders into the bright morning light. Was it still only morning? It felt like they'd been in darkness for two days.

Jess kept walking, her hold on him propelling him forward, as though Jedidiah marched behind her with a gun jabbed in her back.

He allowed himself a glance over his shoulder to make sure that wasn't actually the case.

No one followed.

Gil kept silent as she led him away from the cave entrance, straight toward the edge of the trees lining the base of the next mountain over.

At last, when they'd taken several steps into the shelter of the woods, she slowed, turning to face him as she exhaled a long breath. "I'm sorry." She spoke barely above a whisper. "I didn't expect Jedidiah to be there." Worry lines etched under her eyes.

He brushed a stray lock of hair from her forehead. "It's all right. We got through it."

She gave a weak smile that was more of a grimace. "Usually, he's with Father. I thought the two of them would be making plans for while Father leaves with us."

He tried not to show his own worry. "Do you think it's bad he knows you took me into the caves?" How much of her fear was paranoia instilled by her father, and how much was due to true danger?

She sighed, her gaze drifting past him. "I hope not. Father didn't tell me not to. He allows me to tend the men who are sick or injured, so I have to make rounds to learn who needs help." Her eyes met his again, unease swirling in their depths.

"But you're still worried." He didn't state it as a question.

She nodded, her teeth tugging at her bottom lip. "Jedidiah...he has a way of twisting things, of making even the most innocent actions seem sneaky."

He swallowed against his tightening throat. They *had* been trying to sneak. From Mick and Jedidiah's perspective, Gil could be planning to hurt their operation. At the very least, he planned to take away one of their workers and steal back hundreds of thousands of dollars' worth of sapphires they hopefully had stored around here somewhere.

He intended to take down part of the evil kingdom they'd built in this mountain wilderness.

First, Sampson.

"I need to find a way to speak with my brother. Is there a time when your father and Jedidiah would both be occupied? The noon meal maybe?"

She shook her head, her eyes going wide. "Not then. Father will expect you at the table to eat with him. If you're not there..." She trailed off, but he could imagine the consequences she feared.

"But didn't you tell Ezekiel you would come by to tend to him then?"

Her mouth pinched. "I usually serve Father's meal, then go check the men. Father will expect *you* to eat with him though."

The alarm in her eyes made his chest ache. What had her father done to her to plant such fear? He wanted to ask her, but the timing didn't feel right. For now, they needed to make a plan for him to see Sampson.

But later, when they had a chance for more relaxed conversation, he needed to know what Mick McPharland had done to such a precious woman. Gil swallowed the bile in his belly. Hearing what had been done to her would surely stoke his anger, but he couldn't help to ease her worries until he knew their root.

"All right." He gentled his tone. "I won't do anything to put you at risk. Where do the men sleep?"

Her lips pressed. "There's another cavern on the east side of the mountain. It serves as their bunkhouse." Her eyes pleaded. "But Gil, there are other men to worry about too. Jedidiah has eyes and ears everywhere. I don't even know them all."

They'd placed their bunkhouse in a cavern too? He couldn't imagine a life where men never left the darkness of those caves —not to work or sleep. What had driven Sampson to choose this existence over their ranch? It couldn't be for the fortune— they all had as much as they could want from their own sapphire mine.

Independence then?

A flash of anger surged through him, directed at their older brother Jericho.

Gil had warned Jericho this would happen if he didn't loosen his vice grip on their younger siblings. Things had seemed better these past couple years since he'd married Dinah, but apparently not enough for Sampson.

Gil had to get to him. He'd offer to help him start over some-where else, somewhere he didn't have to live like a cave rat.

He'd sneak out tonight and find Sampson. He wouldn't tell Jess though—it would only worry her more.

Forcing a reassuring smile, he gave her hand a small squeeze. "It'll be all right. We'll figure something out." Even as the words left his mouth, he prayed they held truth.

Lord, guide my steps. Help me reach Sampson and get him out of this place. And keep Jess safe.

As they emerged onto the path, the rugged face of the moun-tain loomed before them. Somewhere inside those dark tunnels, his brother toiled.

Gil's jaw tightened. One way or another, he would find a way to help Sampson. To bring him home.

No matter how hard that goal became.

~

Surely, it had to be midnight.

Gil eased his bedding aside and sat upright, listening for McPharland's steady snores. The man had been sleeping for at least an hour now. No one could fake those snuffles and wheezes. God willing, the man wouldn't wake.

Jess's steady breathing in between her father's racket proved harder to hear, but he caught pinches of it as he pushed up to a crouch.

He still, waiting for a reaction from the woman sleeping on the narrow bed beside where he lay on the floor. When her breathing remained steady, he grabbed his boots, then stood, not daring to breathe. He tiptoed in his stockinged feet, carrying his boots as he slipped around the curtain and across the open stone floor to the exit. The sparse furnishings in this chamber made it simple to keep from running into anything.

As he eased past the exterior door curtain, a chilly wind swept over him, carrying the scent of earth and pine needles. He slipped his boots on, then paused to let his eyes adjust to the dim moonlight filtering through the trees. Jess had said the bunkhouse was located on the east side. It would be a shorter distance to go right, but it might be better to go left and circle around the base the way she'd taken him the other times. With a deep breath, Gil traced their steps from earlier, hugging the base of the mountain as he crept.

The rough stone scraped against his shoulder when he passed the western entrance, concealed by the cluster of cedars. A few minutes later, he reached the southern opening where they'd entered earlier that day, between the two boulders. He slid a look to his right, toward the woods she'd led him into so they could talk.

In the scant moonlight, nothing moved.

He picked his way slower now, since he didn't know the terrain. The grass grew higher here, covering low boulders. In the shadows from the quarter moon, it became hard to tell the difference between soft underbrush and unforgiving stone.

More than once, he misjudged a shadow. One time in particular, he stepped over what looked like a rock, and his footing gave way into the soft grass. He stumbled, scrambling with his other foot for purchase. His toe struck hard stone, jabbing pain through his leg.

He bit back a grunt. As he regained his footing, a whisper cut through the night air, so faint he might have imagined it.

"Gil."

He froze, his heart hammering. *Had* he imagined the sound? It might have only been the rustle of grass.

Then a shadow moved by the rocky cliffside, and a figure separated from the stone.

He made out the familiar shape of Sampson in the darkness. Gil's breath rushed out as relief sagged his body.

What was his brother doing out here?

Sampson motioned for him to follow, then turned and walked away from the mountain.

Gil trailed him, keeping his steps light. They wound through clumps of trees and around low boulders, keeping the mountain's ominous presence at their backs.

Finally, Sampson stepped behind a large boulder, tall enough to hide both of them, even when standing. When he turned to face Gil, moonlight reflected in his eyes.

Gil soaked in the sight of him, but spoke quickly, keeping his voice to a whisper. "How are you?" Sampson had bulked more through his shoulders—heaving a pickaxe everyday would do that to a body, though he'd been muscled enough to start with.

His brother shrugged, but his features remained guarded. "Fine."

That hardly seemed possible after his time here, but they had no time to argue. Not tonight.

"We don't have long," Sampson said. "What are you doing here?"

"Looking for you, obviously." His heart pounded from the tension of trying not to be discovered. "I've come to get you out of here."

Sampson crossed his arms and tilted his head, a wry smile playing at the corners of his mouth. "You had to get married to do that?"

An image of Jess flashed through his mind, with her startling beauty—the way he first saw her on the side of the mountain. Despite everything, he couldn't help grinning. "The opportunity fell into my lap."

As quickly as the smile came, the reminder of Jess's father swept away every happy thought. "I promised Jess I would get her out too. But I need to know some things first." Best to start with the most important question. "What does Mick McPharland do that keeps everyone here living in terror?"

Sampson's face hardened into a grim line, and he spat onto the ground. "He's a cruel man. Jedidiah's no better." He gazed back where they'd come from, but the boulder obscured their view.

When Sampson turned to him again, his focus held steady. "I watched Jedidiah shoot a man dead in the mine the day I got here. The poor fellow asked a question. I never heard exactly what he'd wanted to know."

A shudder ran through Gil at the picture formed. The last thing he wanted was to imagine his little brother witnessing such a horrible act.

"That wasn't the only time," Sampson said. "I've heard

rumors about them killing family members of men who dared to run."

No.

Was that why Sampson stayed? Gil had to get him out. Surely all the Coulters together could protect their family from the reaches of Mick McPharland and Jedidiah.

"No one leaves once they've started," Sampson said, answering his unspoken question. "Some of it's the pay, which is decent enough. But mostly, they stay out of fear." His gaze bored into Gil's. "Everyone's afraid Mick will hunt them down or find their families if they try to leave."

The words churned in Gil's gut. He swallowed hard and forced the next question out. "What about Jess? What does he do to her?"

"His daughter?" Sampson shrugged, dropping his gaze back to the ground between them. "I don't know much about her situation."

Frustration pressed through him. Not that he would expect Sampson to know her well. But did Jess have no one she could confide in? No one who helped her?

Maybe Ezekiel?

Sampson lifted his eyes again. "I've never spoken to her, but she comes up here once or twice a day. She only talks to the men who are sick or injured, and Ezekiel tells her who they are."

He would have to learn Jess's secrets from her then. But one thing Sampson might know... "Have you found the sapphires they stole from our ranch?"

Sampson's eyes narrowed. "Forget about those." His gaze hammered into Gil. "They're not worth getting killed over." He nodded toward the mountain behind them. "You take your new *wife* and get out of here as quick as you can." He paused to swallow hard. "Pretend you never heard of Mick McPharland."

Gil clenched his fists to keep from grabbing his brother's

shoulders to shake some sense into him. "I'm not leaving without you."

The sapphires didn't matter, not compared to convincing Sampson to flee. "Come with me. You don't belong here."

His brother wouldn't meet his gaze now.

Gil pressed. "Don't you want to get away from here?" *Please say yes.*

But when Sampson finally looked up again, he shook his head hard. "I can't leave yet."

Yet?

"Why not?"

Sampson took in an audible breath, then let it out slowly. His voice was so low, Gil barely heard the words. "This is the place I have to be right now. To learn what I need to."

What kind of answer was that? "Learn what?"

Sampson shook off the question. "Take the girl and go."

He started forward, past Gil and around the boulder the way they'd come, and Gil shifted to follow. Just before Sampson stepped into view of anyone who might happen along, he faced Gil one last time. The hardness had left his expression. "It's good to see you, Gil."

If only the circumstances could have been different.

Gil's throat ached. "We miss you. Everyone's worried."

A hint of a smile tugged at one corner of Sampson's mouth. "Tell them I'm fine. Now go on home." With that, he turned and walked back toward the mountain.

Gil had no choice but to do the same.

CHAPTER 10

*J*ess soaked in the aroma of frying bacon as she turned the strips in the frying pan the next morning. So far, Gil and her father still slept. She didn't have to wonder why Gil was extra tired this morning.

When he'd slipped from his covers in the night and crept out of the cave, she'd followed of course. She'd expected him to search for his brother.

And Sampson had already been up to meet him.

Had they somehow scheduled the meeting? Or were both so desperate for conversation with the other that they'd had the same idea without planning it?

She'd crept close, straining to hear their words, but only caught snippets—*sapphires* and *wife*.

Did *wife* mean her? Possibly. Sampson must be curious how his brother could be suddenly wed to his boss's daughter. Had Gil told him the truth?

Her middle tightened. They'd not discussed whether anyone should be brought into confidence about their pretend *union*. It might be all right if Sampson knew. But what if he told someone else, someone who reported back to Jedidiah?

Jedidiah would tell Father, and not only would Father be livid—possibly enough to harm Gil. He would also force her to marry Stuart Wallace.

Father's snores ceased. He'd be coming soon.

As she selected the portions of bacon and potatoes he would like best, the rustle of her own bed curtain sounded.

She glanced over as Gil pulled the cloth aside and stepped out. He still wore that sleepy look, his hair tousled and his eyes squinting a little.

Her heart pumped a little faster.

He was so handsome, but in the morning before he came fully to life, something about him made her want to plant a kiss on his cheek. Actually, she'd much rather press her lips to his— they looked so full and supple right now. A peck on the cheek would be more acceptable though, given their situation.

As though he'd heard her thoughts, Gil walked right up to her, not stopping beside the stove but moving behind her. When his hands rested on her sides, she froze. All except her heart, which surged like a runaway horse, pulling free of the bit in a reckless gallop.

Gil's stubble-roughened jaw brushed against the sensitive skin beneath her ear, and his warm breath caressed her cheek as he pressed a lingering kiss there.

She'd been right. His lips were full and supple this morning.

"Good morning, wife." His voice graveled in that sleepy tone that made her knees weaken. If not for his hands at her sides, she might melt into a puddle right there.

She wanted to lean back into his solid warmth, to lose herself in his embrace, but a thud from Father's room startled her back to reality.

Gil's hands fell away, and he stepped back just as Father emerged, yawning.

"Morning," Father grunted, his gaze flicking between them with a sharpness that belied his sleepy appearance.

Jess turned back to the stove, focusing on dishing up breakfast with hands that trembled more than they ought.

Gil returned Father's greeting, and the chairs scraped as the men sat at the table.

She brought over their plates at the same time instead of bringing Father's meal and coffee at the same time. Would he notice the change? The way she was elevating Gil to the same preference she gave Father?

Gil met her eyes as she set his plate in front of him. That warm brown gaze held hers as a smile curved the corners of his mouth. "Thank you."

Father picked up his fork and speared a potato. "Bring me some coffee, daughter."

With effort, she broke the connection with Gil, then turned to retrieve both mugs. Was it worth riling her father to make it clear Gil's importance in her life? He needed to believe their story. Yet, she knew well the danger in angering Mick McPharland.

After filling her own plate, she sat at the table with the men. Gil had said he wanted her to be part of meals, so she might as well join them before he had to ask her to. When she was settled at her place, she realized what a treat it was to eat at the table while the others did, not steal snippets of bacon in between her work while her father ate. It wasn't as hard to relax with Father when Gil was also here, his comfortable gaze flicking to hers, the hint of a smile when their eyes met.

Throughout breakfast, Father peppered Gil with questions about his family and life on the ranch. Gil answered in his usual easygoing manner. He'd told her about his brothers and the wives of the three older ones, but she hadn't heard about all the other people who lived on the ranch. His niece and nephew, the sister of his brother Jericho's wife, as well as the sister's husband and their two daughters.

It must feel like a small town with so many of them.

She couldn't imagine having so many women close by. Were there rivalries and gossip, or did they get along like best friends? Would they welcome her? Or keep her at a distance? They were all family, after all.

She'd always wanted a sister, someone who would be a friend she could confide in. Yet, she'd also learned things often didn't turn out the way she imagined them. If for some unfathomable reason she were settled near Gil's ranch, having his sisters-in-law nearby could be frustrating or downright miserable.

Or, it could be everything she'd ever dreamed.

"So, what are you two planning for today?" Father dropped his fork beside his empty plate and leaned back in his chair.

His words tightened a knot in her middle. His expression didn't hold censure, but she knew well he was asking because they'd gone in the caves yesterday—an action that she hadn't mentioned when he'd asked their plans yesterday morning.

She worked for a casual tone. "I need to get back to those winter shirts I was making. We might take the work down to the creek where the lighting is good."

Father's eyes narrowed. "Might want to stay out of the caves then."

She nodded. "Of course."

He pushed to his feet. As he pulled his hat from the hook, he gave his usual farewell. "I'll be back for the midday meal." Then with a final glance around the room, he stepped around the door curtain.

She eased out a breath and stood, gathering the used dishes to keep her hands busy. She had plenty of work to accomplish.

But as she loaded the plates into the wash bucket, Gil stepped up beside her and took the rag. "I'll wash these."

She slid a look at him. "This is my work."

The corners of his eyes creased as he reached into the bucket and pulled out a cup. "I'd like to." Now his mouth curved upward. "Makes me feel right at home. Back before Dinah and Naomi came, we boys had to do the cooking and cleaning ourselves."

She couldn't find a single word to answer him. Father never would have dreamed of helping with women's work. But she also couldn't bring herself to push Gil away from the bucket of soapy water.

So she turned her focus to cleaning the stove. Cooking bacon always meant she needed to wipe down every inch of the cast iron.

They worked in easy quiet for a few minutes, the only sounds the splashing of water and the clink of dishes.

"Think you could show me the men's bunkhouse this morning?" Gil asked.

Jess slanted him a sideways glance, lifting her brows. "Didn't get to say all you wanted to your brother last night?" She kept her tone light, but her heart picked up pace.

Gil stilled, his hands braced on the wash bucket as he turned to her. "You know about that?"

Should she tell him she'd followed him? So far, Gil had given her no reason to distrust him. In fact, he'd gone out of his way to help her, even at his own peril. "I followed you. I saw you talk with Sampson, but I didn't hear what you said."

The corners of his mouth twitched as he turned back to his washing. He didn't speak for a moment, clearly focused on his thoughts. "It was good to see him." His voice held a wistful tone.

She searched for a response to keep the conversation going. She wasn't good at small talk. She just didn't have enough experience with it. "Is he excited to leave?"

Gil's mouth pressed, and his brow wrinkled. "Says he doesn't want to go. That his work here isn't done."

Jess tried to make sense of that. Why in the Montana Territory would Sampson want to keep working in these caves? Working for Mick McPharland. Most men tried everything they could to leave, but Jedidiah forced them to stay.

Gil shrugged as if hearing her thoughts. "I've no idea why, but I aim to find a way to talk him into leaving."

A new concern niggled through her. She'd not thought about how Sampson would leave. She and Gil would depart with her father, of course. But should Sampson sneak away during the activity around their departure? Should she tell her father the men were brothers so Sampson could ride out with them?

No.

Revealing that connection felt far too dangerous for both Coulters, if her father hadn't already realized it.

Her stomach tightened. If he had, the fact that he'd kept silent about knowing the men were brothers couldn't bode well.

Yet if her father was unaware, the very last thing she wanted was to bring the fact to his attention.

She'd finished with the stove and moved to wipe the table as Gil carried the wash water outside to dump.

Father had all but told them not to venture into the caves today. But Gil wanted to see the bunkhouse. And the rebellious part of her wanted to show it to him, despite her father's words. Maybe they could sneak in and out without anyone knowing.

When they finished their work, she dried her hands on her apron. "I can take you to the bunkhouse. There's a tunnel that leads there."

He nodded, his gaze wary. "Will that cause problems?"

She shrugged. "Not if we don't meet anyone along the way."

He inhaled a long breath, then let it out in a slow stream. "I'm ready when you are."

Now would be as good a time as any. After slipping past the door curtain, she pointed Gil to the right instead of moving toward daylight. Shadows hid the black curtain covering the inner passage, so one would have to be looking for it to see.

Gil's gasp behind her showed he must not have seen it before now.

She didn't dare speak to him—even a whisper might make too much noise, and this was the passage her father used all the time—but the tunnel was so dark that she needed to lead Gil so he didn't stumble. She reached for his hand, her fingers finding his arm and slipping down to catch hold around his palm.

She wouldn't be lighting a lantern, no matter what.

The warm strength of Gil's hand around hers settled her nerves as they moved deeper into the mountain. He'd learned to walk much quieter through the darkness than he had that first time she led him to the large cavern to look down at his brother. Had that only been two days ago? It felt like he'd been here for weeks.

She kept her senses straining for any sign of approaching men. The brush of leather against rock or the faint glow of a lantern ahead. They passed both storage rooms and the turn-off to the caverns, and then the tunnel opened into the bunkhouse, a long low room lined with cots. She halted to let Gil see the space.

His gaze swept over the scattered belongings and rumpled bedding. She should release his hand. With daylight coming through the open entrance, she didn't need to guide him any longer. But she couldn't bring herself to let him go.

But he pulled away, moving toward one of the cots in the center. He seemed caught in his thoughts as he reached out to touch a shirt draped over the end. "This is Sampson's." His voice came quietly. "One of his favorites."

He lifted the shirt, staring at it for a long moment. His Adam's apple bobbed as he swallowed hard, then he set the garment back down.

She moved to his side and studied the worn yellow cloth. She could almost imagine Sampson wearing it while he worked in the hot sun on a ranch. What kind of life had he known before coming here? Before being drawn into her father's dark world?

She glanced up at Gil, and a knot formed in her throat as emotions played over his face. How hard this must be for him, to be so close to his brother and yet unable to convince him to leave this dangerous place.

After a minute, Gil turned back to her, a shadow in his eyes. "Wish I'd brought a note to leave for him. Something to persuade him to go with us."

If only she had the right words to comfort Gil. But what could she say? That Sampson would surely come to his senses? She had no way of knowing if that were true. Her father held a powerful sway over the men who worked for him, either through fear, manipulation, or a twisted sense of loyalty. Breaking free of that grip was no easy feat.

He swallowed again, determination slipping into his gaze despite the weariness there. "I'll find a way to talk to him again. To make him see reason." He glanced around the dim bunkhouse. "Might have to come back here after dark, when everyone's asleep."

Her gut twisted at the thought of him sneaking around at night again. He might meet one of the guards next time.

Urgency pressed in her chest. "We should head back." No sense in taking extra chances now.

Gil turned around the way they'd come.

When they reached the dark tunnel, she paused to take his hand. He placed it solidly in hers, wrapping his strength around her. His eyes had lost their sadness, restoring the glimmer of warmth. How did he shake off his burdens so easily? Was he that good at pretending?

Yet it didn't feel like pretending. The way he gave her hand a gentle squeeze, the way he held her gaze so easily, the smile creases so ready at the corners of his eyes...it felt like he truly had faith that this would all work out.

Lord, I want that too.

She led him through the dark tunnel.

One thing at a time. For now, she needed to gather her sewing and take Gil out to the waterfall. An hour of sitting beside the peaceful flow always eased her spirit.

CHAPTER 11

*G*il strode beside Jess as they trekked through the woods. Either she was slowing down, or he'd learned to match her quick, long strides, for he could finally keep up with her. As they maneuvered the pine-needle-covered path, he drank in as much of this wilderness beauty as he could.

The sun shone bright, though it's warmth was weak since they were moving into winter. Around them, pines so abundant and tall, reaching up to the heavens as if in constant prayer. Rocks and fallen trees lay scattered between the upright trunks, and in the distance, the rocky cliff of the next mountain over showed through the woods.

A rumble of water grew louder as they reached a clearing beside the creek. The waterfall wasn't tall, about half his height, falling to a pool that flowed into a stream. This was a soothing place, the peace of it weaving through him and easing the tension in his shoulders.

Jess dropped into a seated position on the mossy ground, her back against a boulder. The rock was just wide enough for him to lean against if he sat close to her. Perfect.

He settled, his shoulder brushing hers. Feeling her warmth

through his sleeve and breathing in the slight scent of lavender that always surrounded her made it hard to think about anything else.

She pulled out the blue cloth she'd brought and extracted a needle from the material.

He should work on the task he'd brought too.

He pulled out the small notebook and pencil he'd carried with him from home. He'd used them to write names and details in his search for Sampson, but now that he'd found his brother, he'd sketch the tunnels.

Jess leaned in. "What are you doing?"

He moved his hand so she could see his drawing, careful not to shift his arm away from the pressure of hers. "Sketching the mountain and caves."

Her brow furrowed, then her gaze lifted to his face, searching. "So you can figure out how to get your brother out?" She seemed worried, probably wondering if he planned more than he'd told her.

Guilt pressed in his chest. He did have more in mind than she knew. Did he dare speak of it?

She was so beautiful, and despite the strength she wore like armor, she seemed almost fragile, her skin as clear as Anna's porcelain dolls, her cheeks flushed in the sun. And worried.

He was the one who'd planted that worry just now, though he'd vowed to protect her.

He needed to tell her everything. He thought he could trust her. Besides, she needed his help to escape her father. And he probably couldn't accomplish what he needed to without her help.

"My brother, yes. And..." How to tell her about the other? Taking a deep breath, he met her gaze head-on. "Your father stole something from my family. Or at least, his men did. Sapphires, a lot of them. I came here to get my brother back—and to get our sapphires back."

Her curiosity shifted to stoic, her expression giving away nothing of her thoughts.

He gave her time to work through all the pieces of the puzzle she'd not yet known.

Her gaze drifted to the waterfall. What had been a peaceful silence moments before was tense now, and the splashing water didn't ease it.

"I didn't know about that." Her voice was barely audible above the falls. "But I'm not surprised. My father..." She trailed off, shaking her head slightly. "He's capable of so much worse than I ever wanted to believe."

Gil's heart ached for her, for the pain this knowledge must bring. He wanted to comfort her, but how?

He slipped his hand over hers, wrapping his fingers around her palm. Her skin was so soft, a fact that always surprised him. And made him want to protect her more. "Jess, I'm sorry. I didn't mean to upset you. I just...I thought it wasn't fair to keep it from you."

Her blue eyes shimmered when she faced him. "I'm glad you told me. It's just...hard. I'm sorry he hurt you. Hurt your family." She gave a sad smile. "I'm surprised you'd be willing to help me, now that I know what my father did to you."

He started to protest—why would he hold her father's actions against her? But she wasn't finished.

She took in a breath that lifted her shoulders. "And I suppose I should mention that it's all right if you agreed to help me just to get closer to my father and have a better chance of finding what he took." Her eyes narrowed a little, but not in suspicion. More like determination. "I'll do everything I can to help. You have my word."

He hated for her to think him so calculating, so bent on doing whatever it took to accomplish his purpose. His mission had been *part* of his reason for agreeing to their fake marriage, but *she'd* been the other part. He needed her to know that.

He squeezed her hand. "Jess, I won't deny that your promise to take me to my brother played a part in my agreeing to help you. But that wasn't the only reason. From the moment I first saw you on that mountain, I knew you were different. I knew I wanted to know you better. And when you said you needed help, there was nothing that would have stopped me from doing all I could."

Her eyes widened, as though she struggled to absorb his meaning. Her hand had gone limp in his. Was it really so hard to believe a man would put her before his own plans? Maybe she'd never experienced that.

He stroked his thumb over the back of her hand. "*You* are special, Jess McPharland. I realized that from the very beginning."

Her eyes turned glassy, and was that a tremble in her jaw? *Oh, Jess.* Every part of him wanted to pull her close, but she already looked like she was fighting emotion. Would she welcome his comfort or push him away?

She inhaled and straightened her shoulders, a forced brightness entering her eyes. "Thank you. And I'll do everything I can to get your sapphires back." Her brow wrinkled. "When were they stolen? Do you think he still has them? Would they be sold by now? Is there a way to track them?"

He kept her hand. "Over two months ago. It was a full wagonload of crates, each packed tightly with gemstones. He wouldn't be able to sell that many sapphires here in the territory. We have a friend in Fort Benton watching for a shipment he might be sending east. We think it's most likely he's storing them somewhere around here, maybe selling them a little at a time or waiting until we've given up the search to send them to the big buyers in New York."

She squinted like she was sorting through what he'd said. Maybe trying to think of places McPharland might have stored them?

She picked up his notebook and opened to the page with the map of the caves. "There are two storage rooms I know of. Here and here." She placed her fingers along the tunnel they'd traveled an hour before.

"We passed them this morning?" He'd not seen anything in the blackness. What else had he missed?

"They've been there since I was young. There's a door and a lock on each one."

His heart quickened. "Is there a way we could search them? Or at least walk that tunnel with a lantern?"

She frowned. "That's the main route my father and Jedidiah use. I don't think it'd ever be safe to be obvious about traveling through there."

"What about at night?"

She shook her head. "Jedidiah roams at all hours. I hear him and Father talking sometimes about things he's seen and heard when he decides to take a stroll because he can't sleep. I think it happens often."

Frustration churned in Gil's chest. There had to be a way. Could one of them watch for Jedidiah while the other searched the cave?

"Maybe..." Her word trailed off.

Hope lifted its head within him. "Maybe what?"

She looked hesitant. "Both of them usually accompany me to town to guard me. I could say I need an urgent trip to the store before we set off. But I doubt Father would let you stay here while we go."

The hope eased its head down as he mulled through all angles of that idea. "I'd be surprised if he allowed a trip at all when we're getting ready to leave. Wouldn't he just say you can stop at a mercantile in the first town we come to?"

Her gaze turned sly. "He would. But I've learned through the years how to talk him into what I really need."

He raised his brows. "Like?"

She tucked in her lips, looking a little nervous. What had she done?

He hoped she would tell without him nudging her along.

She shot him a nervous look. "When I was sixteen, Father arranged for me to marry. It was someone he knew, a man he'd done business with."

Gil's middle churned, pulling so tight he could barely breathe.

How could a father do such a thing to his daughter? Only sixteen? Too young to be married off to a man she didn't love.

Maybe it wasn't her age at the time that bothered him most. The thought that she could belong to another man ignited a fire of jealousy inside Gil.

But she wasn't married—*Thank You, God.* How had she gotten out of it?

She stared at the flowing creek. "I didn't know the man, and I sure didn't want to marry him. I guess that was the first time I realized my father might see me as something other than his daughter. That I was a possession to him, someone he could use for his advantage." Her mouth formed a pained smile.

"Anyway." But her voice shifted to a forced lightness. "I was allowed to meet him once, a few days before our wedding. He was..." She wrinkled her nose, sliding a quick look at him. "... not what I was hoping for. He reminded me of Jedidiah a little. Taller, but just as conniving. Older than me, of course, maybe by fifteen years. Which might not have been a problem." She shrugged, as though she wasn't speaking of a very narrow escape that might have changed her life forever. "I could've lived with it if he were someone I could respect. But I would have been a possession for him, too, something he'd paid good money to obtain, to be used when and how he wanted."

Her mouth pinched. "I knew I had to get out of it. So I convinced my father I was too young to marry. That I hadn't yet reached womanhood..." A blush turned her cheeks and ears pink. "That my husband would be unhappy with me and likely demand his money back. I described how much worse things would be for him, how he'd lose respect from those he does business with."

She let out a breath. "It worked. He called the marriage off. I think he even got the fellow to carry on with one of the schemes they'd plan to do together anyway."

Gil's mind whirled.

How could any man not treasure her? Especially her *father*, the one man she should always be able to depend on. The man who should make her feel protected and cherished.

Anger burned in his belly.

He had to get her away from Mick McPharland, no matter what else he accomplished on this mission. And he wouldn't send her off into the wilderness to fend for herself, either. If he could talk her into staying at the ranch, he'd do it.

Dinah would welcome her into their home, he had no doubt. As would any of the other women.

Jess needed to know what it meant to feel safe, to *be* safe. To be part of a family who cared abut *her*, not what she could do for them.

And was it too much to hope she might one day fall in love with him? Because he was more than halfway in love with her. He didn't want to confuse love with concern, but she ignited something deep inside him. Something solid that hadn't been there before. Like part of him had been searching and had finally found its perfect match.

Jess smiled, the look almost sly—but in a sweet way.

If that even made sense.

"I think I could convince my father to take me to town if I had to. I could make him think there's a way he'll benefit from the trip." Her voice turned hesitant. "If you think that would be helpful."

"I don't want to use you like that." He shifted away, turning to face her, and held her eye contact. "I'm sorry your father did. I promise I never will. You're safe with me." He infused meaning into his words and hoped she saw sincerity in his eyes. "When we're back on my family's ranch, you'll be safe there too. No one will make you do anything you don't want to."

Wariness flashed in her gaze. Did she not believe him? Or did she worry about going to their ranch?

He'd have to cross those hurdles later.

He settled beside her again, enjoying the feeling of her shoulder against his, her hand in his.

It was amazing that such ugliness—her father, his business, these caves—could coexist with the beauty of this place.

How could they explore the tunnel without being caught?

He mulled the question. "If we had a couple of lookouts, we could search the cave where the storage areas are." He angled toward her and found her watching him. He wouldn't define the look in her eyes, needing to attend to the problem at hand, but if he were to define it...

Wonder?

He swallowed emotion that crawled up his chest. There was nothing *wonderful* about him. He was just a man who knew how to treat women. The fact that she was so surprised by him wasn't so much about his—for lack of a better word—*goodness*, but about her father's ugliness. And that of all the people he'd chosen to surround his daughter with.

Focus, Coulter.

Right.

"Sampson and your friend Ezekiel. Could they distract your Father and Jedidiah?"

Fear flitted across her gaze. "No. Nobody talks to Dad or Jedidiah unless they have to. They'll punish a man for the tiniest infraction."

Gil didn't want to put his brother or that godly old man at risk. "What about at night? Where does Jedidiah sleep?"

"He has a chamber off the side of the bunk room."

Another hidden room Gil didn't know about. How many more could there be? He'd have to talk through the map with her and see if she remembered any other spaces, no matter how insignificant.

But an idea was beginning to form.

"Maybe tonight when both of them should be sleeping, we can ask Sampson to help. He can stand inside the tunnel near the bunk room and give some kind of signal if Jedidiah comes out. Do we need a lookout at the other end for your father?"

Doubt gathered in her expression. "Probably not."

Probably not.

Should Gil ask Ezekiel so they could be certain? Bringing in another person would add to the risk—that they'd get caught, or that someone could get hurt. Maybe she could watch for her father and distract him if he started to leave the cave

Sampson wouldn't like the plan, but he'd go along. Gil just had to find a way to ask. "Are you going to tend to Ezekiel while your father and I eat at midday?"

She gave a wary nod. "He was in a lot of pain yesterday."

"Could you slip a note to Sampson, or put it under his blanket?"

She let out an exasperated breath. Clearly, she understood his plan and it didn't sit well with her. "I suppose." Her brows gathered in a frown. "The sapphires might be somewhere else. I need to think about it."

"All right."

She pushed to her feet. "I want to check on a flower I found on the other side of the waterfall before we go back."

He stood, too, as she stepped to the edge of the bank, then onto a flat stone that poked up above the water's surface.

As she moved to the next rock, he scanned the opposite bank for what flower she meant. A low bush with bright green leaves sat at the base the falls. Purple flowers peeked out from the leaves. It wasn't a plant he'd seen in this area, and it was lovely. No wonder she liked it.

Jess threw her hands wide, and his gaze snapped to her.

She yelped and tumbled sideways into the water.

"Jess!" He lunged forward, his heart leaping into his throat. Could she swim?

CHAPTER 12

*P*anic flooded Gil as the water covered Jess. For a frantic moment, fear paralyzed his mind. Had she hit her head and drowned?

But then she rose so both shoulders cleared the surface.

Relief crashed through him, overpowering every other emotion.

Water streamed down her face and hair. She pushed the wet strands back, wiping liquid from her eyes. Only when her face held the hint of a smile did he let out a breath.

He reached down to help her out. "Are you all right? What happened?"

She took his hand and let him help pull her up the steep side of the pool. When she reached dry ground, she collapsed to sit in the moss. Her skirts hung limp, fully drenched and probably heavy. Her shirtwaist clung to her, outlining every one of her curves.

He forced his gaze back to her face as he crouched in front of her. "Did you slip on a rock?"

"Went lightheaded. My vision blackened for just a second. By the time I could see again, I was already toppling."

Concern clenched inside him. "Why? What's wrong?" Was she ill? Did she have a disease she hadn't told him about? Maybe from living in that cave without enough sunlight.

"Nothing's wrong. I don't think so, anyway. This has happened a couple other times since I learned about the baby. I remember my mother saying she swooned once when she was carrying me."

Baby.

He froze. Was she saying...? His mind reeled as he tried to process what she meant. "Baby? You're...with child?"

Her eyes narrowed, confusion gathering in her brows. "I told you I was. When we spoke to my father."

His body finally thawed enough that his heart surged, hammering through him. "I thought it was a desperate ploy to make him see he had no choice but to accept we were married." His legs could no longer hold him, so he dropped to sit on the ground beside her. He couldn't pull his eyes from her though, even as he tried to wrap his mind around what her revelation meant.

Who was the father? *Where* was the father? Why hadn't he married her? And not just as a pretense.

How far along was she?

A new thought pressed in, smothering out the rest as anger roared back to life. Had someone accosted her?

She placed her hand on his arm. "I'm sorry I didn't make it clearer before. Everything happened so fast, and I..." She trailed off, looking out over the water.

He searched for something to say. His muddled mind couldn't find a coherent word.

"I need to get back. The food."

He leaped to his feet before she could untangle her sodden skirts enough to stand, then gripped her arm to help her balance.

Clearly, she didn't want him asking all the questions that

hammered him. Maybe, hopefully, if he gave her space, she'd tell him in her own time.

She sent him a quick smile before pulling away and striding back the way they'd come.

As he followed her to the cave, one thought finally came clear amidst the muddy mess of questions. The stakes in this mission had suddenly become so much higher. He had to get Jess and that tiny life inside her to safety. No matter what it took.

~

*L*ater that afternoon, Gil scrubbed the last of the dishes, his thoughts a whirlwind. Sitting beside Mick while they ate the midday meal had been just short of torture, especially with Jess gone to tend Ezekiel. Gill had disliked her father when he'd arrived, but he was coming to loathe the man more every day. Which made being civil to him just a hair shy of impossible.

Now Mick had finally gone back to his work, and Jess hadn't yet returned.

The water sloshed around the tin plate as Gil worked off the remnants of their lunch.

Knowing about the babe didn't change his plans where she was concerned. He'd still get her out of here. Still help her settle on his family's ranch. Still do his best to make her love him as much as he was coming to love her.

But he had so many questions about how she'd come to be in her condition. What he needed to ask might not make for polite conversation, but he had to know. Especially considering how invested his heart was in her already.

Did she love the father? Or did she bear scars from an ordeal Gil could hardly stand to imagine?

He needed to know. Everything in him wanted to pull her close and protect her.

He rinsed the dish, then set it on the towel to dry.

A rustle by the door had him turning in time to see Jess slip in. His chest tightened, both at the fresh blast of her beauty and what he had to say.

Her eyes were wide with excitement though. She glanced around the room. "Is Father here?"

"Nope." He dried his hands on the cloth. "He went back to work."

Her eyes sparked with a light he'd rarely seen there. "I remembered another storage room." She moved toward the curtained area where they slept. "I tried to get in, but it's locked. I think I can open it though. I just need something."

Turmoil twisted inside him. He was desperate to ask his questions, but if they had a chance to find the sapphires, they couldn't waste it.

He followed her to their sleeping area. "What can I do?"

"Get another lantern. We might need more than one." She motioned toward the cluster of them hanging near the door.

Within minutes, they slipped out of their home, and she led him around the base of the mountain, where they entered the cave she'd brought him to the day they'd first met. She lit the lamps just inside the entrance.

He kept his voice low. "Are you sure it's safe to have lanterns?"

"This tunnel is rarely used anymore. It was the first passage Father found when he started mining this mountain."

Jess led the way, moving slowly enough that he was able to study the walls on both sides. This did appear to be a natural cave, at least the first part. Now that he looked closely, he could see where the natural cave ended and tools had been used to chip away the rock and carry the tunnel onward.

Ahead, Jess had stopped to study the wall. As he neared, he

noticed an outline in the rock. A stone door? It must be incredibly heavy. On the left side halfway between the low ceiling and the rough floor, a round lock protruded a little from the stone.

Jess crouched on the right side though. Down near the bottom… Was that a hinge? A glance upward showed another near the top on that side.

He dropped to one knee next to her, bringing his lantern close so she could see better. There was a difference in coloring between the wall and the door. In fact, the door looked… painted?

He touched the surface, which was a rough texture but not cold stone. Definitely painted. And was that…? He made a fist and knocked.

Wood.

What remarkable camouflage. In the dim light of the tunnel, even carrying a lantern, he would have passed this twenty times before spotting the lock or hinges—if he'd ever seen them at all. The hinges and handle had been inset as much as possible, the wood meeting the stone around it so cleanly, that the seam was barely visible.

"It's so hard to see, I often forget it's here." Jess was picking at the hinge with the metal hatpin she'd brought.

It had been fastened from the inside, making it secure. But Jess had poked the tip of her hatpin into the narrow opening between the door and cave. "I saw my father do this once when I was a girl. I remember being curious about how he'd managed to take the door off the hinge, so I looked at it from the inside later. I think I can remove the inside pin. It just might take a minute."

All Gil could do was watch while she worked.

Her face twisted as she worked, her brows lowering and her mouth puffing out on one side like she was biting her tongue. Adorable. And she was so smart. This woman had lived a life no young girl should be forced to endure, but she'd come through it with intelligence and savvy.

How could he not admire her?

Her expression brightened as she leaned in to exert more pressure. "I think..." Her face fell as frustration snuffed out the hope. "I lost it."

She readjusted the angle of the hatpin, and her mouth twisted again.

He could start on the upper hinge if he had something pointed like her hatpin. His pocketknife had an edge, but not a round point like her tool. He could try.

As he started to rise, metal clattered on the other side of the door.

"Got it." She pushed the bottom corner of the door, and it wiggled a little. Not much, but more than it had before.

She stood, hatpin in hand, and reached up to the top hinge.

"Let me try that one? Might be easier for me." The hinge was at his eye level, but she'd have to stretch to reach it, which would surely hurt her arms after a minute.

She didn't hand him the hatpin, just kept on with what she'd been doing. "Let me fit it in the notch between the pin and hinge, then you can work the pin up."

Less than a minute later, she stepped back, holding the hatpin secure in the crack with one hand. "Careful not to dislodge it. You have to be really gentle. Just a slight wiggle until you get the pin loose."

As he placed his hand over hers and she pulled away, he did his best to keep the hatpin still. He needed to get a feel for how much effort he should apply to make it wiggle. She was right though. He had to use the slightest of movements or the tool would slip out of the crack between the hinge and the hinge pin.

Jess was trusting him—even though a man might struggle with such a delicate touch. From the corner of his gaze, he checked her expression.

Hopeful. Maybe a bit nervous. He would prove worthy of her trust.

It might have taken him a little longer to release his hinge than it had her, but at last he worked the pin high enough that it fell out of the hinge.

He blew out a breath as he lowered his arms.

The door shifted a little, but not much.

"We should be able to pull it out of the lock." She mimed sliding the wood to the right, probably pulling the lock bar out of its secure setting in the stone.

He placed the hatpin and both lanterns behind them so he'd have room to maneuver the door.

Jess was already there, trying to pull it, but her arms barely extended the width of the wood.

He bit back a chuckle. "Can I try?"

She stepped away to allow him room. In the hinge side, he could now work his fingers in the crack between the door and frame, but he had to pinch the edge of the wood to pull it enough to create a finger space on the lock side.

When he did, he gripped the door with both hands and slid it sideways.

The lock bar pulled free, and he moved the door fully out of the way, resting it against the cave wall.

His heart hammered as he reached for his lantern.

Jess already had hers and was stepping into the doorway.

He stood beside her, lifting his lantern high to take in the sight before them.

Crates piled all the way to the ceiling, just taller than Gil. Some were slightly smaller, but most looked very familiar.

He stepped closer to touch one. He and his brothers built the crates for their gems, and didn't mark them until they were ready to be shipped. Even then, they'd usually be labeled as potatoes or pickles or some other relatively heavy staple that shouldn't stir undo interest.

But these...they had to be from the Coulter mine. He could see at least five crates that looked like theirs. Adjusting his lantern, he pulled one down from the top of a stack and placed it on the floor. The lid had been nailed shut, but everything about the outside proclaimed it to be from his family's mine. He had to know if the sapphires were still inside though.

Jess watched him without speaking.

He gripped the edge of the lid and pulled upward, working the nails loose. He opened the lid enough to expose the contents.

A layer of black felt lay on top.

Jude always packed their gems in black felt.

Gil lifted the fabric, bringing the lantern closer to make out the rich blue of the stones inside.

He'd found his family's stolen sapphires.

CHAPTER 13

*G*il's chest clutched so tightly he couldn't breathe.

He'd done it. He'd actually found his family's sapphires. He'd been determined, but deep down, he'd feared he'd never see them again.

He forced the air from his lungs as he replaced the felt, then the lid. He lifted his gaze to the mountain of boxes in the storage room.

"The gems in that crate are yours?" Jess's voice was low.

He nodded, keeping his gaze on the other boxes. "My family's."

"Do you think they're all here?"

Good question. He returned the crate to its stack and raised his lantern to see to the rear wall. He couldn't see how many rows back the boxes went.

"How large is this cavern?"

"Not far. Father parked our handcart in here once. He had to push it all the way to the back to close the door."

Which meant the entire wagon load of crates stolen from their mine couldn't be in here, not with the number of other boxes visible that weren't theirs. *Probably* not theirs anyway. He should check at least one to make sure some of the Coulter sapphires hadn't been repackaged.

He hoisted down one of the smaller boxes. It was made from a different wood, which didn't hold the nails as tightly. He pulled the top off to reveal a wad of gray cotton material.

Inside were gemstones of several different colors. Mostly red, but a few yellow and green. Sapphires could be different colors, though blue was the most common. They'd not mined any red last year that he could remember.

The contents of this crate must be from a different source. Possibly still stolen, though.

He replaced the lid and pushed it down with his knee to drive the nails back into the soft wood, then lifted the crate back to its place.

From her spot at the doorway, Jess gave him space to think and move.

He stepped back and eyed the full storage room again. "Without digging all the crates out and opening them all, I'd estimate this is a portion of what was stolen. Maybe up to half." He peeked over his shoulder to catch her reaction.

A frown lowered her brow. "Could the others have been sold already?"

"I don't know anyone in the territory who'd want or be able to afford so many sapphires." He tipped his head. "I don't have your father's contacts, though. We always ship ours east to sell."

They should close up this room and get out of here before someone found them. He glanced at the lock. "Any idea where the key is for this? It'd be nice to get in here a little quicker next time."

She scooped up her hairpin and stepped closer to the door. "Let's leave it unlocked. My guess is no one will notice for the few days we'll need."

Jess turned the lock on the door in the corridor quickly—she sure had a talent with that hairpin—then he lifted the thing and positioned it so she could fasten the hinge pins. At last, they closed the door, pressing it into the firm fit that concealed it well. He pushed on the handle a little to make sure the door would open again—which it did—then snatched his lantern and turned to Jess. "Can you think of any other rooms off this corridor?"

"I've thought about that. There's nothing." She started toward the exit, and he stepped in beside her. They'd taken a half dozen steps when a figure appeared in the shadows ahead.

His heart surged into his throat.

The figure took on the shape of a small man. As he moved closer, the lantern light glowed on Jedidiah's face.

Jess had frozen beside him. She pressed a hand to her chest, letting out an audible breath. "You scared me, Jedidiah."

His compact features wreathed into a smile that showed his teeth. A creepy look, especially with the light casting deep shadows on his face. "I would have made a noise if I'd known you'd be here. I didn't expect you to directly disobey your father. What do you think he'll say about that?" Even his voice sounded sinister. On purpose, no doubt. He was intentionally planting fear in Jess.

Gil stepped forward. He'd gladly call the man's bluff. "Her father didn't forbid her from entering the caves, and we didn't hinder your workers. We didn't even see them." Gil took Jess's arm, tugging her forward. "The architecture in these tunnels is amazing. You and your men have done well with them." He guided Jess past the little bully, who glared at them. "Good day."

He kept Jess moving, though she seemed sluggish. He shifted his arm around her back so he could give support. Was she trembling?

They needed to get out of this tunnel.

By the time they reached daylight, she was vibrating with fear.

He didn't stop at the entrance to leave one of the lanterns

there. He could take it back once Jess was better. Just now, he needed to get her to a safe place where he could comfort her, somewhere Jedidiah couldn't follow.

Because Gil had no doubt the man *had* followed them.

He could take her to the waterfall, but the man could still creep behind them and watch. Besides, she might need to lie down and rest. Her cave-home would be the best place, as long as her father wasn't there.

He'd have to take that risk and change plans if McPharland appeared. She certainly didn't need the stress of facing her father.

Jess had tucked herself into his side, and he held her close as they walked up the hill around the base of the mountain. She hadn't spoken, but her trembling had turned so severe it almost felt like convulsions.

When they reached the apartment entrance, he nudged the curtain aside with his shoulder, glancing inside to see if McPharland was within. No sign of him.

Gil led Jess forward, and finally her trembling seemed to ease. A little. Should he take her straight to bed? Maybe. He needed to know why Jedidiah frightened her so much. What had the man done to her to create such intense fear?

A thought flashed through his mind that made his breath catch. Could he be the father…? No, surely not. *God, don't let that be what happened.*

Jess reached for one of the chairs at the table. "Just let me sit. I'll be fine."

She probably needed to rest, but it might be best if she reached that conclusion herself. He helped her settle in the chair at the table, then pulled another around beside her.

She leaned against her seat back, her arms wrapped around her waist, eyes straight ahead. Her mind seemed held by the clutches of memory. What memory?

He brushed a loose wave of hair from her temple, and her

eyes closed. He let his fingers linger there. His callused skin was coarse against her softness. "Jess." He kept his voice as low and comforting as he could. "Can you tell me why Jedidiah scares you so much? Did he hurt you?"

He wanted to cup her cheek, but she needed comfort right now, not romantic touches.

So he slid his hand down her arm to wrap his fingers around hers. She met his gaze, and so many emotions swirled in her eyes that he could barely discern them.

Lingering fear certainly. And maybe a bit of desperation. She was trying to regain control of herself. The way her jaw tightened and her throat worked showed that.

"He's cruel. He's never done anything directly to me, but he's threatened me. And I've seen him punish the others. And I've heard...far worse." Her voice cracked on those last words.

Gil's chest was still tight, but less now that she'd said that slimy man hadn't done what he'd feared. Still, he had to be sure.

He gave her hand a squeeze. "Are you sure he's never touched you? Never hurt you in any way?"

She shook her head, not looking away from him. But the sorrow filling her eyes turned the edges of them red. "Not me, but so many others."

He could breathe again. Thank God.

But Jess's distress grew, and he could keep her at arm's length no longer.

He pulled her closer, and she came willingly, tucking her forehead into the crook of his neck and resting a hand over his heart.

He wrapped her tight as a sob slipped out.

His own heart threatened to crack from the pain she was feeling. How much had she seen? Had she been close to the people Jedidiah hurt? *Lord, comfort her. Bring healing to replace her grief. Show me how to help her.*

She only let herself cry a minute before pulling back and

wiping her eyes with her sleeves. She likely needed to release a good many more tears than these, but at least she'd allowed a start.

She sniffed as she dried her cheeks again. "I'm sorry. I don't usually break down like that."

He offered a smile. "Don't be sorry. I'm here any time you need to break down."

She made an effort at matching his smile. Would she try to change the subject now? Pretend the tears hadn't happened? She'd likely had a lot of experience covering up her pain.

But when she spoke, a glimmer of hurt flashed in her eyes. "I guess I should be as concerned about Father, but I haven't seen Father hurt people as much as I have Jedidiah. Only one time, and that was so long ago." She gave a slight shrug. "It's easy to forget about that and just think of him as my father."

From what he'd seen, she still feared McPharland far more than a daughter should her father, but he didn't need to point that out. If the man had raised her so separate from the rest of the world, he could make her believe the most heinous actions were perfectly normal.

Yet, somehow, she'd developed a sweet and loving spirit.

Jess's gaze turned distant. Was she remembering when she'd seen her father hurt someone? Or some other awful action she'd been forced to watch? Had her father or Jedidiah forced her to watch the men's punishments? Or had she seen accidentally? Or sneaked in and peeked from a hidden position?

Knowing Jess, that seemed likely.

"When I was seven, there was a man who worked for my father." Her volume was low, her words coming slowly as if she chose each with care. "I never knew his name. He was kind to me, though, always had a smile and a treat for me when I saw him."

Her throat working. "One day, I accidentally knocked over a lantern where the men were working. It shattered, and an ax handle caught fire. Father was furious. He thought the man had been careless."

Tears welled in her eyes again. "I tried to tell him it was my fault, but he wouldn't listen. He dragged the man outside and..." Her voice cracked and she pressed a hand to her mouth.

Gil held her to his chest, his heart aching for the traumatized girl she'd been. "You don't have to say more," he murmured against her hair.

But she shook her head and pulled back to meet his gaze, a fierce light in her blue eyes despite the tears. "No, I need to tell you. You need to understand what he's capable of." She drew in a breath that lifted her shoulders.

"Father called Jedidiah, and together they beat that man. Beat him until he was barely recognizable. And Father made me watch, saying it was my punishment for lying. That I needed to see what happened when people were careless in their words and deeds or didn't do what they were told."

Fury warred within Gil's spirit. What kind of monster would do that to a child? To anyone? He fought to keep his voice steady, to not let his anger show. "Oh, Jess. I'm so sorry. No one should ever have to see something like that, especially not a little girl."

She gave a jerky nod. "I know that now. But back then, I didn't understand. I thought it was my fault." Her shoulders slumped. "I still do sometimes. If I hadn't been in that room, if I'd pushed harder for Father to believe I'd broken the lamp—"

"No." Gil cupped her face, holding her gaze. "None of that was your fault. Your father is the only one to blame. He's a cruel man. You were an innocent child."

A single tear escaped down her cheek, wrenching his heart. "Sometimes, I can still hear that man's screams. I can still see the blood..."

She closed her eyes, squeezing them shut, and Gil gathered her close again. If only he could wipe away those memories.

She buried her face against his chest, and he stroked her hair, wishing he could wipe away every hurt she'd ever experienced.

"I've got you," he whispered. "You're safe now. I won't let him hurt you ever again. I won't let Jedidiah hurt you either. I promise."

If only Gil could stop the men from their cruelty to others.

Once he had Jess to safety, maybe he and his brothers could come back and stop Mick McPharland for good.

He held Jess for a long time, her slight frame wracked with silent sobs as he murmured soothing words. His mind raced with this new insight into the hell she had endured. The strength it must have taken for her to survive. Where had her mother been during that awful scene?

The few times Jess had spoken of her mother, they sounded like fond memories. But what kind of woman would marry a man like Mick McFarland? Maybe she'd been forced into the arrangement and never found a way out.

He pushed out a tight breath. He wouldn't let that happen to Jess, no matter what.

CHAPTER 14

*G*il had no idea how much time had passed when Jess straightened from against his chest. Her red-rimmed eyes showed just how hard this afternoon had been for her. "I told you that so you would know how dangerous they are. Jedidiah and my father." Though no fresh tears tracked down her cheeks, grief and sadness filled her tone. "We can't make a wrong step, Gil, or they'll hurt you. I thought…" Her voice faded, but then it gained strength. "I'd thought if you were married to me, you'd be protected. But if he stole from you… Father's greed more than trumps whatever affection he has for me."

Gil had to take the weight of this worry off her shoulders. All these years, it must have smothered her.

He tapped the tip of her nose with his finger, a touch that hopefully came across as playful. "Don't worry about me, Jess. I can handle them. I promise."

The apprehension didn't leave her eyes, but that tap on her nose brought his focus a little lower. To her lips.

He jerked his eyes back up. She needed *comfort* right now. To know she was safe. Not amorous advances.

But her expression had shifted to something more...aware. Her gaze flicked down to his mouth and hovered there. She rolled her lips in, her tongue peeking out between them like she was moistening them.

Aw, man. What was he supposed to do with that?

She'd appealed to him from the very beginning, even in the general store, and when he'd caught sight of her up on this mountain, she'd seemed like an angel.

An angel he'd just been holding in his arms. Their emptiness felt stark now, cold after the warmth of her.

Did she want him to kiss her? Would it resurrect awful memories of another man? That thought alone held him back with an iron chain.

Yet her eyes held no sign of fear. If anything, they'd darkened with desire. She leaned forward a little. If he read her right, she welcomed him.

He couldn't take advantage of her, certainly not when she was so vulnerable.

He brushed his fingers over her cheek, relishing the softness of her skin. "Jess, I want to kiss you." Talk about an understatement. "But I won't unless you want me to."

A hint of question crossed her expression, but not fear. She regarded him, those wide blue eyes so beautiful. So rich. She seemed to be searching for something. For his motives? He could talk for days about why he wanted to kiss her. But maybe she just needed to know if she could trust him. She would need to see that for herself.

At last, she gave a tiny nod. "I do."

The iron chain holding him back turned to warm butter, but he forced himself not to dive in. Not to scare her. This woman deserved to be treasured. Cherished. And he would show her what that meant.

He cupped her jaw with tender fingers, brushing his thumb over the full line of her bottom lip.

A shiver ran through her, making it even harder for him to move slowly.

He leaned in, little by little, and she met him partway. With less than a handsbreadth between them, he paused and searched her eyes, waiting. Noticing the flecks of gold and brown in her irises.

She had the feel of innocence about her. It was her smooth skin, unmarred by too many hours in the sun. It was the openness in her gaze. It was the hope that seemed to shine from within, despite all she'd endured.

But it was more than that. She seemed fragile, like her heart would wound if he didn't handle her with the greatest care. She was somehow as strong as the walls of the cave she called home —and as tender as the newest blooms of spring.

He closed the final space between them and brushed his lips across hers, as gentle as he could manage.

The contact sent a flame through his body.

Her lips were pillow-soft, warm and yielding beneath his.

He lingered there a moment, then went back for another, careful not to move too quickly. He wanted her to know his feelings for her went deeper than any kiss could convey.

The third time, he tilted his head more to deepen the kiss, sliding his hand back to thread through her silky hair.

She sighed, her own hands coming up to rest on him, one against his chest and the other on his shoulder.

Her earnest response stirred hunger inside him. It took every ounce of his willpower not to respond the way he wanted to. But forced himself to stay tender and reverent, pouring into his kiss all the feelings he couldn't yet put into words.

When they parted, they were both breathing heavily. Gil rested his forehead against hers, his eyes closed, relishing the feel of her. The warmth of her breath on his skin.

"Jess." Somehow he needed to tell her what she meant to him. What her trust meant to him. "I—"

"Well, isn't this cozy." A sharp voice cut in, shattering the moment.

Jess jerked away, and Gil faced their interruption.

Mick McPharland stood in the doorway, arms crossed, eyes fierce.

Gil stifled the urge to cower and apologize. As far as McPharland knew, his daughter was Gil's wife.

Maybe the man would rather not walk in on the scene, but he had no right to be angry about it.

And Gil wouldn't cower before this man.

Jess scrambled to her feet

Gil rose and faced McPharland, stepping between Jess and her father.

"Hello, sir." He worked for a pleasant expression. "You're back early."

McPharland's scowl darkened, and he pushed off the rock wall to step forward. "I heard the two of you were wandering my caves again after I told you not to. I didn't expect to come back to find you halfway between the sheets."

Jess's gasp did more to stoke Gil's ire than her father's demeaning words.

He wouldn't allow this man to insult her, nor would he let her feel shame over what they'd just done—a simple kiss. A kiss he didn't regret.

He straightened to his full height, making him, taller than her father, but kept his tone steady. McPharland would pounce if he thought he'd poked hard enough to draw blood. "Sir." The word came out with just the right tone. Clipped, yet not disrespectful. "I can't allow you to speak of my wife in such a crude way. She deserves respect from us both."

The air in the room had grown thick. He wasn't touching Jess, but he sensed she would be quivering again.

McPharland was building a head of steam from Gil's words —his red face made that obvious.

Gil motioned toward the doorway. "Maybe it's best we step outside to finish this. Jess needs to rest." He started forward, but McPharland sliced a hand through the air to halt him.

His voice turned cold. "Don't forget whose house you're in, boy. I can make things very unpleasant for you."

"For *us*, you mean?" Gil posed the question to remind the man who he was. "You would threaten your son in law because I dare to kiss my wife?"

The man blinked, then sidestepped to focus on her. "What were you were doing in the caves?"

Gil shifted toward her.

She looked like a doe facing a hunter and his loaded rifle.

He needed a good answer, now.

"We meant no harm. Gil wanted to see the bridge again. We were only there a minute."

McPharland glared between them again, and Gil fought the urge to step in front of Jess once more.

The man's eyes narrowed on Gil. "I'm no fool. You were searching my mine. Looking for your brother, were you?"

Gil's insides plummeted.

When had the man learned of the connection between him and Sampson? Had he realized it from the beginning? Gil might as well come clean on that part.

He dipped his chin in a single nod, not losing McPharland's gaze. "I *am* looking for him. Sampson Coulter. I heard he was working in these parts. Working for you." He kept those last words even and respectful so as not to stir the man's anger again before this final request. "I'd like him to come with us back to the ranch."

Gil didn't realize his hands had fisted until Jess's fingers brushed his wrist, nudging where his fingertips bit into his palms. He slipped his hand around hers. The contact settled him, easing the whirling in his mind.

McPharland's eyes flashed with a cold, mocking amusement.

"You think Sampson wants to go back with you? That he's being held here against his will?" He shook his head. "Your brother is right where he wants to be, doing exactly what he wants."

Gil kept his voice steady, though it took effort . "I'd like to hear that from him, sir, if you don't mind. Surely you wouldn't deny a man the right to speak to his own flesh and blood."

McPharland's mouth twisted in a sneer. "I'll ask Sampson if he wants to see you. But don't get your hopes up." He shifted his gaze to Jess, his expression not softening the least. "I'm moving up the timeline. We leave day after tomorrow. First light."

Gil's pulse surged.

That left him only a day and a half to get the sapphires out and convince Sampson to leave too.

McPharland turned on his heel and stalked out, leaving a heavy silence in his wake.

Gil exhaled a long breath, giving Jess's hand a gentle squeeze. Tears glimmered in her eyes, a sight that made his chest clench.

"Jess." He reached for her, needing to feel her, to comfort her.

She came into his arms willingly, burying her face against him as she had earlier. He stroked her hair, murmuring against her temple. "It's all right. I've got you. He won't hurt you, and he won't hurt me. I promise."

She nodded against him, but tension vibrated through her.

He eased his upper body away so he could see her face. He cupped her cheek, brushing away an escaped tear with his thumb. "Listen to me, Jess. God has control of this situation. No matter what happens, no matter what your father says or does, God can overcome it. With His help, I'll take you somewhere safe. My family's ranch if you'll go there, or anywhere you want. I promise, I'll make sure you don't ever have to live in fear again."

Though apprehension still lurked in her eyes, trust crept in now too. Trust in God hopefully. And in him.

He had to live up to that trust and keep this most important promise.

CHAPTER 15

*J*ess worked the dough, kneading and forming each roll until she had a full pan ready for baking. She'd already filled the oven with as many pans of bread loaves as it would hold, so these rolls would have time to rise before their turn in the oven. Bread seemed the best staple to hold them as they traveled. And she'd have a wedge of cheese and slices of ham for sandwiches.

The methodical work helped settle her mind, but her spirit still swirled with too many emotions to count.

Gil sat at his usual place at the table, writing something in his notebook. Or maybe drawing. Working on his sketch of the mountain with all its caves? He kept glancing up at her, as if he wanted to help or something.

She needed this time. Time to gather her nerves. Even when he'd offered to take over stirring the soup, she'd refused.

She caught him watching her again. "What?"

He blinked. "Nothing."

"You keep looking at me like you want to say something."

One side of his mouth tipped up. "Not really. I just..." He shrugged. "I'm glad you're feeling better. You seem to be enjoying whatever that is you're baking. And it smells like heaven."

She smiled, warmth spreading through her chest. "It's just bread and rolls. Nothing fancy, but it should keep us fed on the journey."

His presence lingered in her awareness as she worked the dough like a comforting embrace. Having him near made everything feel more bearable somehow.

A few minutes later, footsteps sounded as the door curtain swished to the side.

Father returning for the evening meal.

She glanced up as he entered, and thick tension came in with him. His expression was impossible to read.

Gil closed his notebook and tucked it in his pocket, then rose, maybe in respect. Maybe to be ready for another onslaught of Father's anger.

"Smells good in here." His voice came out gruff as he hung his coat on its peg. He took his usual seat at the table.

"Bean stew and sourdough rolls." She ladled the soup, then placed the rolls still warm from the oven on plates in front of each man before gathering her own food.

They ate in strained silence for a few minutes, the only sounds the clinking of spoons against bowls.

Father spoke casually, as if commenting on the weather. "That old miner you're so fond of...they say he's dying."

She froze, her spoon halfway to her mouth. "What? Who do you mean?" She lowered her spoon, her mind racing to make sense of the words. "Not Ezekiel?"

It couldn't be.

He'd been fine when she stopped by to rub liniment on his back at noon. Well, not fine exactly. In pain, but not...dying.

Father shrugged. "I was told he's breathing his last."

Panic spurted through her, and she sprang from the table. "I have to go to him." She spun and started for the door.

"I'm coming too." Gil's words made her freeze, and she turned back to check Father's expression. He wouldn't want Gil in the bunk room with the other miners.

But Father waved a dismissive hand. "Jedidiah's there." Father spoke around a mouthful of bread.

She eased out a breath. Not that seeing that weasel made her feel better, but at least Gil would be by her side for this.

She grabbed her shawl from a hook and snatched up a lantern.

After shrugging on his coat, Gil took one of the extra unlit lamps, and she led the way to the tunnel. At the threshold, she reached for Gil's hand. This lantern peeled back some of the black, but she'd rather have his strength.

He gripped her solidly, and they hurried through the corridor, the glow from their lights bouncing off the rough stone walls.

Storage rooms flashed by at the edge of her vision, but she didn't spare them a glance. She had to get Ezekiel before it was too late. By the time they reached the bunkroom, her lungs burned, and a stitch stabbed her side.

Several men were huddled around Ezekiel's bed, and her middle turned queasy.

It was true. Father was right.

But maybe he'd exaggerated.

She forced her leaden feet to carry her forward.

Sampson was one of the men gathered, and he stepped back to make room for her and Gil.

Dropping to her knees at the bedside, she met Ezekiel's wonderful, familiar gaze. But his eyes held no shine. She took in his ashen face, his papery skin, and the way his chest hardly seemed to rise, though the rasp of his breathing sounded loud in the quiet room.

Tears stung, but she held them back. "What's wrong,

Ezekiel?" She touched his shoulder, the one she'd rubbed liniment on just hours ago. "What's happened?"

His mouth curved, though it seemed an effort. "Don't you worry...Miss Jess." He stopped to catch his breath between the words. "My lungs are...jest tryin' to get...the better...o' me."

She rested her hand atop his. "Don't speak. Let's get some licorice tea in you, and you'll feel better, like always." But he'd never been this sick before. Surely, he'd need more than licorice tea.

At least he wasn't coughing.

She turned to one of the men on the opposite side of the bed and pointed to her satchel of medicines she kept hanging on the wall in the corner. "Could you bring that to me please?"

A fierce cough erupted from Ezekiel.

She startled at the sound, turning back to him.

That first hack turned into a fit, each cough surging from deep inside him, wet and thick. His body didn't stop to let him breathe, and panic clamped her insides. Were these to be his final moments?

She scooted behind him and forced her arms under his shoulders. "Help me. Someone."

Gil was already on the other side of the bed, lifting the older man, bearing the brunt of his weight. When they had Ezekiel to a sitting position, she managed to say, "That's enough. Hold him here."

The way Ezekiel's shoulders lurched with every deep bark, he wouldn't be able to hold himself upright. *Please, God, don't take him now. Make them stop.*

At last, the coughing subsided, and Ezekiel sucked in tiny, ragged breaths. Her own heart finally resumed beating, yet watching him suffer with each intake made the tears press hard again.

"We need more pillows." Her voice shook. "To prop him up."

Men scrambled to gather bedding, and soon they had Ezekiel resting in a more upright position.

Gil stayed on the other side, keeping the patient from sliding back down. Ready for anything.

This bunk room was always quiet, the men usually too weary from the hard work to be raucous. But now, a suffocating pall hung over them all, no one moving or speaking except when she asked for help.

She took her satchel from the man who'd retrieved it, not even looking to see who it was, and rummaged through the contents. Where was the pouch of licorice? There. "I need a kettle of hot water." She opened the drawstring and pulled out the thimble she used to measure it. "Put a full scoop of this in the pot." She thrust it toward the nearest man.

Sampson.

He took the pouch and thimble and moved toward the cookstove.

She turned back to her satchel. She'd already spotted the cough syrup. Uncorking the bottle, she poured a generous dose into a spoon, then raised it to Ezekiel's mouth. "Can you drink this?"

He parted his lips and swallowed the liquid with a grimace. The expression added a bit of life to his face, easing the weight on her chest a small bit.

What else could she do for him? A peppermint poultice for his chest?

Before she could move to prepare it, Ezekiel rested a hand on her arm. The weight of his touch made her pause, and she met his gentle gaze.

"It's all right, Miss Jess," he rasped out. "It's my time. The Lord's callin' me home."

"No." The word burst from her, her heart crying out. "You have to fight. I can help you get better, I know I can."

But even as she spoke, the words rang hollow. The truth of

his condition settled like a boulder in her gut. He was dying, and there was nothing she could do to change that.

His hand tightened on her arm, drawing her eyes back to his face. "The Lord...numbered my days...afore I was born. Ain't nothin'...you can do...to change that."

A sob welled in her throat. She captured his large, callused hand between hers as the tears she'd been holding back spilled free. "Please don't go. I can't lose you too."

Ezekiel had been her rock, her anchor, for so long. The one person she could always count on, who taught her about the Lord's love and showed it to her every single day. He'd been more a father to her than her own had ever seemed. The thought of facing this cold, hard world without his steadying presence...

She couldn't bear it. She dropped her forehead onto their joined hands as sobs took over. Ezekiel's other hand came to rest on her head, his fingers working through the messy strands that had escaped her braid in that soothing, paternal way he had. "Hush now," he rasped.

The calluses on Ezekiel's fingers caught in her hair as he stroked her head, but the familiar roughness only made her cry harder. This dear man had been such a comfort, such a light in the darkness of her life. Losing him felt like losing a part of herself.

Another hand rested on her shoulder. Gil must have moved around to her side, and now draped his arm across her back like a cloak to protect her against the storm inside her. He didn't say anything, just let his touch communicate his support, his presence.

As much as she couldn't face the thought of losing Ezekiel, Gil would be here to help. And God too.

Maybe she should feel peace, but all she felt was the breaking of her heart.

Ezekiel's hand lifted off her head, falling to rest on his blanket.

She straightened and wiped her wet cheeks with her sleeve. As she met Ezekiel's eyes again, peace shone there. The absolute certainty that he was going home to Jesus.

"I love you." She managed a broken whisper. "Thank you. For everything."

He gave a weak version of that dear, crooked smile. "Love you...too, Miss Jess. The Lord's...got His hand...on you. He'll be there...when I'm gone."

Fresh tears slid down her face, but she nodded. "I know."

Ezekiel looked to Gil then. "Take care of...our girl."

Gil's arm tightened around her. "I will. I promise."

With his breath still wheezing with every small inhale, Ezekiel closed his eyes. "I'm tired."

"Sleep now. We'll be right here."

Though his breathing slowed and his hand went slack, she kept holding on. Memorizing the lines of his weathered face, the calluses on his fingers. This man who meant more to her than almost anyone.

Sobs built in her chest again, but she held them in so she wouldn't disturb Ezekiel's peace.

Gil shifted beside her, drawing her closer so she could lean against him.

They stayed like that—Gil holding her, her gripping Ezekiel's hand—as the room grew heavy and still.

The other men faded into the background. All she knew was the man beside her and the one slowly slipping away.

Finally, with one last rattling sigh, Ezekiel went still.

An awful feeling settled over her as she held her breath, watching, waiting. But his chest didn't rise again.

Anguish built in her, ripping from her throat in a cry.

Gil pulled her fully against him, and she buried her face in his chest and let the great heaving sobs come.

He was gone. Her friend, her mentor. One of the two best men she'd ever known.

CHAPTER 16

$\mathcal{G}$il kept his breathing steady as he stared up at the darkness from his bedroll.

Jess and her father were both asleep, surely.

It'd been awful seeing her after Ezekiel died, holding her as she grieved. Ezekiel was probably one of the only people in her life who'd loved her unselfishly.

When he'd brought her back to the apartment, her father had been waiting for them. His gaze had narrowed as he sat at the table. Thankfully, the man hadn't said much, because Gil wouldn't have put up with his hurtful words.

She'd gone to bed soon after they returned, and Gil had tucked her in. Sleep was what she needed most. His chest ached, and he'd hardly known the old man. If only there were something more he could do to ease Jess's pain. No matter what anyone said or did, the grief would have to work its way through her system over time.

It had taken a long while for her breathing to slow after she'd stopped crying.

Now, he looked one last time at where she lay tucked under blankets on her cot. She wasn't likely to awaken, given how exhausted she must be. Which is why he'd not told her what he was about to do. After tonight, there would only be one more day and night to convince Sampson and get the sapphires out. He couldn't waste any time.

As quietly as possible, he eased up from his bed pallet, picked up his boots, and slipped past the curtain into the main room. McPharland's snores never halted as Gil crept toward the doorway. On the way out, he grabbed one of the extra lanterns and stuffed a few matches in his pocket.

Outside, the cold night air hit him like a splash of icy water. A welcome jolt to his senses after the stifling warmth of the apartment. He pulled on his boots, his fingers fumbling hooks in the dark.

Above him, stars glittered sharp and bright against the inky sky, tiny pinpricks of light that seemed to mock the heaviness in his heart.

He let the chilly air fill his lungs. Then he set off, skirting around the mountain, keeping his steps as silent as he could on the rocky ground. The trees covering the opening to the cave, a darker patch in the night. He'd keep the lantern unlit until he was inside the storage room—if he could make it that far in the dark.

As he slipped behind the cedars' branches and stepped into the shadows of the cave entrance, a voice behind him shattered the stillness.

"Halt!"

Gil whirled, his heart leaping into his throat.

A short, wiry shadow stood five steps away, a rifle pointed at Gil's chest. Jedidiah.

Despite the faint starlight, the man's face was lost in shadow. Yet Gil could feel the weight of his gaze, cold and assessing.

Gil wasn't far enough into the cave that the darkness hid him, so Jedidiah would see any movement he made. Was the man a quick shot? Gil could possibly lunge sideways and avoid the bullet, then attack Jedidiah before he could reload or be prepared for a fight.

But what good would that do, except to bring other men running? He wouldn't be able to get the sapphires out either way, and he might ruin his chance to retrieve them later. He'd likely make it a lot harder to protect Jess too.

So he scrambled for a quick excuse. "I dropped something when we were in this cave earlier." The words spilled out in a rush. "My pocket knife. It's special to me. Just realized it was missing, wanted to find it before I lost it for good."

Jedidiah's silence stretched. When he spoke, his voice carried a cold menace. "Ain't nothing in there worth finding. But I'll take another look for you. Why don't you turn around and go on back to that *wife* of yours? And stay there."

The way he said *wife* made Gil's skin crawl. Did Jedidiah suspect the truth behind their pretend marriage? Gil's mind raced, searching for some way to get past the man, to reach the sapphires. But with that rifle trained on him, he stood no chance. Not tonight.

He nodded. "All right. As soon as you lower that rifle."

The small man didn't drop the barrel, but he stepped back, allowing Gil to slide between the trees and the rock, then start up the hill toward the apartment.

He had to fight to keep from showing his frustration. Especially with Jedidiah's gaze boring into his back like a physical weight.

Once he'd returned the lantern and matches to their places, he settled down on his pallet and stared at the dark ceiling once more.

Time was slipping away like sand through his fingers. One more day and night to get the stolen crates out and loaded on a wagon, then convince his brother to drive it.

He closed his eyes. *Lord, I need Your help. Help me convince*

Sampson to leave this place. And show me a way to get those sapphires out. Give me an opportunity, before it's too late.

The night's silence was his only answer. But he had no doubt God heard him. How He would answer could sometimes look different than Gil expected.

He sighed and rolled to his side, willing his racing thoughts to be still.

Morning would come all too soon. He needed rest, needed to be sharp and ready for whatever challenges the new day would bring.

~

*G*il gripped Jess's hand as they walked in the cool morning sunshine, following a path around the mountain. The path to Ezekiel's grave. She'd not taken him this way before, and he was thankful they didn't have to cut through one of the dark cave tunnels. The mood surrounding them this morning was dark enough. Seeing her good friend's burial would be hard for her.

She turned away from the mountain, and they traipsed through tall grass toward a meadow broken only by scattered clusters of cedars. Between the trees ahead, a few men had gathered. Two still packed dirt on the grave, while others waited in respectful silence.

Sampson was one of the men working a shovel.

Gil's throat tightened. At least his brother still possessed the willingness to do what he could for a friend and neighbor. Had he been close to Ezekiel?

As Gil and Jess reached the group, other men joined them, coming in twos and threes.

Jess's hand tightened in his, and he followed her gaze to the wiry form of Jedidiah.

Gil didn't let his frustration show. At least he'd given Jess room to be with Ezekiel in his last hours without bullying her.

Would he be as respectful now? A glance at his face showed a glare aimed directly at Gil. He must still be sore about their middle-of-the-night meeting.

Gil nodded and faced the grave. He needed to have his wits about him during this next hour.

They all gathered by the burial spot, forming a half-circle around the freshly-turned dirt. The tall trunks of a pine forest lined the opposite side of the grave. At least two dozen men stood here—more than he'd seen in the mine or the bunkhouse.

No one spoke at first, but a kind of hallowed reverence lingered in the air. Should he lead a prayer or a hymn or something? Jedidiah didn't seem like he planned to speak. Was there another leader among the men?

Jess spoke before he could decide what to do, her voice trembling slightly. "Ezekiel was one of the best men I ever knew. He never complained, despite pain that would lay many men low. He was always ready with a kind word or a helping hand. I remember the first time I met him. He was sharing his meal with another man who'd come to us hungry. Along with the food, he shared his stories and his kindness. Ezekiel had a way of making even the darkest days seem brighter, just by being there."

She swallowed hard.

Her father had joined them, standing on Jess's other side. He wrapped an arm around her shoulders and tugged her close.

She ran her thumb over the back of Gil's hand, then released it.

Gil was tempted to push McPharland's arm away from her. The man couldn't choose when he wanted to be a doting father and when he'd rather resort to threats. But Jess seemed to take comfort in having him there, and Gil wasn't about to cause a ruckus during a funeral.

A fellow down the row cleared his throat. "I remember when I first joined up. I was green as grass and didn't know a thing about mining. Ezekiel took me under his wing, taught me everything he knew. Never once lost patience with me, even when I made numbskull mistakes."

Gil scanned the crowd until his gaze landed on Sampson. His brother had backed to the edge of the group, his face an unreadable mask. What was he thinking?

A thought slipped into Gil's mind, faint but insistent.

As men told stories about Ezekiel, he could slip away unnoticed. Maybe Sampson would follow, and they could move the sapphires out of the cave twice as fast.

Would Jedidiah notice them leave? Would Mick?

If the other men did, would they raise an alarm?

The way Jedidiah and McPharland were both focused on the mound of dirt, he could probably shift backward and tuck behind a tree to signal Sampson.

As if God were orchestrating the situation, another miner stepped from the crowd to speak about Ezekiel.

Gil took the chance to shuffle backward, out of the midst of the group.

His brother's gaze didn't shift from the miner, but Gil had the feeling Sampson was tracking his movements.

He jerked his head toward the mountain.

Sampson's brow gathered in curiosity, probably wondering why Gil wanted him to follow. But he nodded, the movement barely perceptible.

Gil stepped back and moved behind one of the bushier cedars so he was hidden from most of the men. He jerked his head toward the mountain once more, making his message clear.

Sampson slipped sideways into a thick cluster of trees on the far side of the semi-circle of men.

They each moved backward, shifting from one tree cover to the next until they'd left sight of the group.

Gil angled to meet his brother, keeping his voice to a whisper. "I need your help to move some crates. Is everyone there at the grave?"

Sampson gave him a sharp look but didn't slow. Would he refuse to help? He'd told Gil to forget about the sapphires, but maybe since Gil had already found them...

Gil kept his voice low. "I know where about half of our sapphires are. I need to move them out to the woods."

Sampson shook his head. "You're asking for trouble." They reached the open area beside the mountain, the massive cliff face looming ahead. Sampson stopped and turned to him. "Where are they?"

Maybe he *would* help.

Gil pointed toward the trail that led around the southern half of the mountain. "On the other side, there's an older tunnel that looks like part of the original cave. It leads to the upper level of that bigger cavern. The storage room is about fifty yards in."

Sampson spun and jogged toward a well-trodden area beside the mountain.

Gil followed, though it wasn't the route he knew.

His brother slipped through a narrow opening in the rock, and when Gil did the same, the bunkroom opened up around him.

Sampson was still jogging. "Come on." He must know a shorter path.

Gil ran behind him through the low cavern, catching up when Sampson paused to grab a lantern and light it. They continued into a narrow passageway, jogging again as they traveled deeper into the mountain. The air grew cooler, the tunnel leading into a cavern—the smaller one Jess had brought him to when he'd first met Ezekiel.

The stab of guilt surprised him, using the man's funeral for his own purposes. But would another opportunity present itself?

Sampson turned toward the corridor that led to the larger cavern, but Gil's gaze sought out the place Ezekiel had been cutting stone. Was that a pick lying on the floor? A weight pressed on his chest.

But he didn't have time to grieve, Sampson had already disappeared into the next tunnel.

Gil lengthened his stride to catch up with his brother, and by the time they emerged into the larger cavern, he was breathing hard.

Sampson aimed toward the far wall to the left of where Jess had shown Gil the stalagmites, just under the wooden bridge that spanned the space above.

Sampson grabbed a rope beneath the bridge. As he pulled it out, the knots tied in the cord became apparent—all the way up to the higher level.

Sampson looked back at him. "The closet's up there, right?"

Gil nodded. It felt like they'd been gone from the funeral a half hour, but this was a shorter path from the one he'd planned to use. And now he knew one more thing about these underground caves, a new way to maneuver should he have the need.

Sampson climbed the rope first, his broadened shoulders rippling under his shirt as he worked his way up. His little brother was little no longer.

Gil followed, the cord biting into his hands with a fury as he used all his strength to climb.

At last, they covered the short distance down the passageway until Sampson paused with the lantern in front of the hidden door.

How had he known it was here?

A question for another time.

Gil tugged on the lock like a handle. Had Jedidiah realized

they'd left it unfastened? Apparently not, for the door shifted when he pulled. He opened it wide, revealing the floor-to-ceiling stack of crates.

One look at Sampson's widened eyes showed he must not have known what lay within.

Gil motioned to their family's crates. "These that look like ours are the only ones we move. The crates that are different stay."

He reached for the crate he'd opened before and slid it off the stack. Could he carry two at a time? Maybe.

He grabbed a second, stacking it atop the first. The weight strained his shoulders and back, but he managed to lift them both, determination fueling his strength. Sampson followed his lead, hefting two crates as if they held feathers.

As they carried the boxes out of the storage room and down the passageway, Gil's mind raced. What if Jedidiah or one of the other men noticed their absence and came looking for them? *Lord, let the men keep telling stories until we're finished.* This might have been a foolish idea, but it was the only opportunity he might have.

They emerged into daylight, and he blinked against the sudden brightness. No one was in sight, so he led the way across an open area into the woods. A few strides in, the underbrush grew thick, and he set his crates down. He could come back and conceal the boxes better once they had them all out.

"I'll bring a wagon here tonight." Gil muttered the words as he struggled to catch his breath. "Load these up, and you can drive it to the ranch tomorrow while I travel with Jess and her father."

Sampson set his load down and turned a frown on him. "I'm not leaving."

Gil started back toward the cave. "We have to get the sapphires back. Please, Sampson, I need your help."

Sampson strode past him. "We don't have time to chatter."

He was right. Gil pushed into a run over the open ground, and Sampson matched his pace.

Together, they made four more hurried trips. That left only two crates remaining from the Coulter stock.

Gil studied what remained. "Let's stack up the rest of these in the front so it doesn't look like anything's missing."

"We don't have time. He's probably realized we're gone."

Gil was already moving boxes, though. It would only take another minute if they both worked.

Sampson jumped in to help, and they got the front row full filled.

"There." Gil blew out a breath. "We'll lock it up, then I can take the last two while you head back."

Sampson led the way out, and Gil pulled the door shut. The lock clicked, and he gave a test shake to make sure the mechanism had fastened. All set.

He turned back to the crates. "Take the lantern with you. Thanks for helping." There was no way he could have moved the sapphires without being caught if he'd had to carry them all himself.

Sampson strode away with the light, leaving Gil in darkness as he hoisted the last two boxes. He'd traveled this path enough to manage without seeing.

As he took his first few steps down the passageway, the space didn't feel as black as usual. Maybe his eyes were growing accustomed.

But then a light appeared around a curve in the tunnel. And it was growing brighter.

CHAPTER 17

*G*il's breath caught, and he shifted backward and to the side so the bend in the wall would protect him from the oncomer's view. Maybe he could move away faster than they were walking. He could stay out of view until... Until he fell off the bridge into the chamber below? Or until he had to try to descend the rope carrying two crates?

Plan B, then. He was trying to figure out what it would be when...

"What have we here?" Jedidiah's voice curled through the cave, tightening every part of his body. Had the man seen him?

He scrambled backward, using the cave wall against his arm to guide him.

"Your game's up, Coulter. You can keep running, but we have you cornered now. And red-handed too, it seems." The man's voice held an irritating combination of high nasal and low menace.

Enough to send a shiver down Gil's back as he set down the crates behind him, then let the light move closer. His heart pounded an urgent rhythm. Would it be better to run? He could probably get down the rope ahead of Jedidiah. But if the man had that rifle from last night—or any weapon—he might use it.

Maybe Gil could bluff his way out of the situation. He could lean on whatever leverage he had as McPharland's son-in-law.

The lantern drew closer, illuminating Jedidiah's wiry frame and those of two other men flanking him. Big men, from what Gil could make out in the shadows. Jedidiah's eyes glinted with a wicked satisfaction.

"What's this about, Jedidiah?" Gil forced a casual tone, as if he had every right to be here.

Shadows from the flickering lantern skewed his predatory smile. "Looks like we caught ourselves a thief. Boss ain't gonna be happy about this, Coulter."

It appeared he wouldn't be able to pretend he wasn't carrying out crates. Maybe a show of bravery would be a better tact. "I'm no thief. Just taking what belongs to my family."

"Is that so?" Jedidiah stepped closer, his henchmen coming too. "Funny, I don't recall the boss saying anything about you Coulters having a claim on our goods."

Before Gil could answer, the man on the left stepped forward. Gil shifted but didn't see the flash of movement from the other guard until it was too late.

A fist slammed into his gut. The air whooshed from his lungs, and he doubled over, gasping as he forced himself back up.

A punch to his face helped raise him, striking his jaw with a crack and whipping his head backward.

Pain roared through him as his body caught up with the blows, but he had to fight. His vision blurred, but he could see the looming outline of a man in front of him.

He struck out, putting force to the blow. His fist hit flesh— but not hard enough.

A jab landed on the other side of his face. His cheek lit on fire and his head pounded.

A boot slammed into his gut, throwing him backward.

He landed on the edge of a crate, falling sideways as he scrambled to pull himself together. His forehead slammed into the stone floor. Pain exploded.

There'd be no fighting his way out of this.

He pulled his knees close and curled into a ball.

A hand gripped his arm and hauled him up.

Gil's body screamed with pain. But he forced himself to open his eyes and see what they would do to him. At least he'd know where the next blow came from.

Jedidiah's face was only an outline through the blurry haze. "If the boss didn't want you kept alive so bad, I'd end you right here." His mocking, nasal tone grated. "But don't worry, we'll make sure you learn your place real good."

Another blow exploded into his jaw, and Gil squeezed his eyes against the pain. The men weren't finished with him, and each punch and kick sent fresh waves of torment through him.

He was helpless to protect himself. They might not plan to kill him, but he felt an inch from following Ezekiel to the grave.

What would happen to Jess? And the baby?

He bent as much as he could with the men still holding him up.

God, help Jess. If you take me away, send someone else to get her out of here.

~

Jess's footsteps echoed through the empty apartment.

Where was Gil?

The funeral had been a blur, listening to all the stories the men told about Ezekiel. She'd been so focused on them, she'd not realized when Gil slipped away.

How had she not felt him leave?

136

Once she realized he was gone, she'd known deep inside what he was doing.

His sapphires.

Why had he thought that was a good idea? Jedidiah surely hadn't missed his exit.

Maybe he'd sent one of his men to follow Gil, for the evil man had stayed at the graveside. Just in case Gil *had* escaped unnoticed, she'd stretched out the service as long as possible, asking for others who wanted to share. Finally, her father gave her a pointed look that said she'd best end things.

Now, peeking behind the bed curtains to confirm the empty beds she'd already checked once, a growing sense of dread twisted her insides.

She hiked her skirts and ran to the door, grabbing a lantern and matches on her way. The sound of heavy footsteps froze her just inside the threshold.

Father never walked with such a loud tread. *Lord, let it be Gil.*

The curtain jerked aside, and Jedidiah marched in, not waiting for an invitation.

Fear surged through her, laced with a fair amount of fury. How dare he enter her home without even knocking? Without asking permission?

But then another man followed—one of his guards—with a limp figure slung over his shoulder.

Her pulse stopped as everything inside her clutched tight. Gil.

No!

A strangled cry escaped her lips. Was he dead? He hung lifeless, draped over the thug's shoulder.

The guard stopped beside Jedidiah in the middle of the room.

The small man's cold eyes met hers, unflinching. "Where do you want him?"

Did that mean he was still alive? *God, let him be alive.*

"On the bed." She hurried to her sleeping area and pulled back the curtains. "Lay him here."

As the guard lowered Gil's limp form onto the mattress, she got a clear look at his face. Bruises and blood mottled his swollen features, and crimson matted his hair.

A sob catching in her throat, she dropped to her knees beside him. *Gil.*

She reached to brush the hair from his eyes but stopped herself. It looked like any touch would cause more pain.

Anger surged through her, shaking her insides as she put the pieces together. She whirled to face Jedidiah, hot tears stinging her eyes. "How could you do this?" Her voice came low but broke with emotion she couldn't contain.

Jedidiah's brows rose. "Caught him stealing from your father. This is what happens to a man who can't be trusted."

Without another word, he turned on his heel and strode out, the guard following not meeting her eyes, though she'd known the man for years. He used to be kind, before. But Jedidiah ruined him like everything else.

Her entire body trembled, but she couldn't let herself fall apart. She had to tend to Gil. If there was anything that could be done, she would do it.

She fell to her knees beside him, watching his chest rise and fall. The movement was faint but unmistakable.

At least one of them was breathing.

She forced air in through her nose, knowing she needed to keep her strength and her focus. Blowing it out, she rested two fingers at Gil's neck where the large artery ran, avoiding a trail of blood that had run from a cut in front of his ear, already drying. His pulse felt as light as his breathing, but the beat ran fast. Was that good? If only she had more medical training.

She knew the little she'd learned from one medical book and the few times she'd been to visit a doctor.

What did Gil need first? The cuts tended to? She had no ice

or snow for the bruising. Were there broken bones? She was out of laudanum, but she had willow bark powder she could brew in a tea. He'd need to wake up in order to drink it.

As soon as Father came in, she would send someone to town for medicine. Until then, best she know exactly what they were dealing with. A quick check of his clothing showed no overlarge blood stains. She pushed up and strode into the main room to gather a bucket of clean water and cloths.

While she tended his obvious wounds, she'd look for broken bones. She'd need to remove some of his clothing to look for bent limbs, swelling, or bruising. Maybe this wasn't proper, but Gil needed help. And she would only check his arms, legs, and abdomen.

She untucked his shirts, lifting the hems of both the flannel layer and his undershirt. Just like a doctor treating a patient.

The first bruise she glimpsed wiped away any thoughts of indecency, honing her attention on what damage might be underneath the skin. The dark purple area didn't appear to be swollen, and it was on Gil's left side, mid-abdomen. From what she could remember of the chart of organs on the wall in Dr. Miskelly's office, only intestines were tucked in that area.

The farther she searched, the more dark skin she found. Almost more than unbruised areas.

One spot above his ribs tightened a knot in her middle. She didn't dare press hard, but she couldn't feel any loose or soft parts of his ribs.

He groaned a few times, deep, heart-wrenching sound, but didn't come awake.

Would she be able to tell if it was broken?

She'd heard that nothing could be done for broken ribs except bed rest. Gil would be in a world of pain when he came fully coherent.

She brushed one light fingertip over his temple in an area

that wasn't bruised or cut. "I'm sorry. So, so sorry." Emotion bubbled up, silencing her.

She pressed a light kiss to that same spot. If there were any way she could take on some of his pain, she would do it.

She rolled up his sleeves and then checked his arms and shoulders without having to remove his shirt. She would worry about his back later.

As for his trousers, should she cut the legs open? She could stitch them back later at the seams. She could probably see almost to his knees by rolling up the hem of each leg, but if there was any injury, she'd need to gain access to treat the area.

For now, best to check where she could under the hems, then focus on washing his face and hair. Just in case she needed to stop a still-bleeding wound.

As she wrung a little water from her cloth to trickle down Gil's right cheek, his eyes opened a sliver. His mouth moved, like he was trying to wet his lips to speak. That would be painful, for both lips were swollen, the bottom one cracked and bleeding.

She rested a finger on his lips, the lightest of touches. "Don't try to talk. I know it hurts. I'm so sorry."

He didn't move his mouth again, but his hand rose from where it lay at his side. Only the hand, as though the arm was too heavy. Or broken? If he could move his hand, the bone wouldn't be fully snapped. She'd check that next.

For now, his eyes had opened wider, his fingers reaching as though he wanted something. The wet cloth? Pain medicine? She still had to brew the willow bark tea, and he probably didn't want the former. Maybe he just wanted a little comfort. This she could give.

She touched her fingers to his palm, and his hand closed around them. Tight. His injuries hadn't stollen his strength—at least not all of it.

140

With her hand firmly in his, he closed his eyes again, and his face relaxed.

CHAPTER 18

*J*ess left her hand in Gil's for a long moment, breathing in the feel of him. He wanted *her* for comfort. Had she ever been so important to another person that just holding her hand brought relief from suffering? Certainly not to her father. The men she treated needed the *medicine* she brought them. Teas for pain or breathing ailments.

Her mother maybe. She'd loved having Jess near anytime she was sick. Not so close that Jess would catch the illness, but in a nearby chair, reading or telling stories. Jess hadn't been there in her last minutes, only Father had. Had his presence comforted Mama?

Jess inhaled a thick breath.

Father was the one responsible for Gil's condition. If he weren't such a hard man, he'd rein in Jedidiah's cruelty.

She couldn't let her mind follow that trail or her body would tense and she'd be no comfort to Gil at all.

She eased the air out, long and slow. Then, one hand still tucked in Gil's, she used the other to lay the wet cloth on his forehead. Better to let the water loosen the dried blood so she didn't have to rub much. She dipped another clean cloth in the water bucket, squeezed it out, and draped it over another part of his face. The cool water might ease his pain a little.

What else could she do? Maybe start willow tea brewing.

She rose to do that, and once she had the water and powdered willow bark heating, she returned to sit on the edge of the bed beside Gil.

When he raised his hand again, she slipped hers into his grasp. What more could she do for comfort? She stroked her free hand over the back of his and hummed a quiet tune.

Her mother had sung this hymn to her often when they worked together, washing clothes or peeling apples. After humming through the verse once, she dared shift to actual singing. Her voice was nothing beautiful, but the words of this song felt so appropriate for Gil's condition. And hers too.

"O God, our help in ages past,

Our hope for years to come,

Our shelter from the stormy blast,

And our eternal home."

She didn't know more than that first verse, so she slipped back into humming.

Gil gave her hand a light squeeze. Maybe embarrassing herself by singing had been worth it.

Did she really believe God would help them? Had He done so in the past? She couldn't say for Gil, but she'd felt the Lord's presence with her this past year since Ezekiel had helped her come to know Him.

Ezekiel.

Tears crowded her eyes once more, and she fought the urge to curl on her knees on the stone floor. How much hurt did the Lord expect her to bear in a single week? First losing Ezekiel last night, and now Gil clung to life.

Her pain was nothing to Gil's, yet her heart felt fractured beyond repair.

She sank to her knees beside the bed, sitting back on her heels as she cupped Gil's hand in hers. She let her forehead drop to the mattress. This wouldn't have happened if she'd been there to help him.

If he hadn't slipped away without telling her what he was doing, she could have stopped him. Found another time when she could have been a lookout for him. Even as the thought rose up, she knew there would have been no other opportunity.

Jedidiah had men everywhere. It would have been impossible to move all those crates without being caught. How much had Gil managed? Any?

Her chest pressed until she could hardly breathe.

This was why she fought to control everything in her life. She had little power over her father and his decisions, but everything else, she *had* to take charge of. She'd learned long ago how much pain came when she didn't—pain to herself and to those around her.

She lifted her head to take in Gil's face, half covered by the wet cloths that had turned pink from the blood. Around the fabric, the bruising made it almost impossible to recognize him, but she knew the man beneath those bruises, the kind, gentle man who'd come to mean so much to her.

Gil.

Hot tears stung her eyes. She'd started to release her heart to him, to let herself trust him. Maybe even let herself love him.

She'd let herself hope.

She should have known better.

Letting go of control brought pain. And this time, Gil would pay for her foolishness.

~

*J*ess studied the slow, even rise and fall of Gil's chest. It'd been at least half an hour since she'd finished cleaning and bandaging his wounds—all except the gash on his cheek that needed stitches. She'd been waiting for the willow bark tea to take effect. It finally seemed to have taken enough edge off the pain that he could sleep.

The damage that remained made her belly churn. Two angry knots rose on his scalp, hidden by his dark hair. A gash on the crown of his head had bled profusely before she cleaned and dressed it. At least it didn't appear deep. But his left eye... The lid was swollen nearly shut, the flesh around it a sickening black. The right eye fared a little better, bruised but not very swollen.

She studied the dark puffy wound that extended from the left eye down to the unnatural bulge along his cheek bone. Were bones fractured beneath that angry skin? She couldn't be certain. And what could be done for broken bones in a man's cheek? Rest might be his only treatment. That and something stronger than the tea to ease his pain.

Despair pressed down on her like a smothering blanket. If only he had never crossed paths with her, he would have been spared this brutality at her father's hands. The suffocating guilt settled like a stone in her chest.

A gash on Gil's jaw needed attention. The cut ran deep enough that it should be stitched. She likely couldn't stop a scar, but maybe she could keep the mark small. She pulled her smallest needle and a bit of thread from her sewing kit.

It took too long to thread the needle, thanks to her shaking hands. She hated stitching skin. Especially since it was usually her father's own men who'd caused the injuries she closed.

Footsteps sounded in the other room, and she turned to face this new threat. She'd tied back her own curtain so she could see when anyone came. Father hadn't yet dared show himself—

probably because he knew she'd be furious—but now that appeared to be changing.

He stepped across the room, his footsteps quiet, his pace measured. His expression looked blank.

No sign of remorse.

Anger boiled inside her. She stood and stepped outside her sleeping area to meet him. She pulled the curtain shut behind her, hoping their voices wouldn't wake Gil.

She leveled a glare on her father. "How could you? Your men beat my husband nearly to death."

His eyes flicked to the curtain, then back to her face. He crossed his arms over his chest, his stance wide and unyielding. "It had to be done, Jess. You know that."

Fury flashed at the edges of her vision. "No, I don't know that!" She had to stay quiet. Poor Gil didn't need her waking him. She breathed hard and forced her voice low. "He didn't deserve this. Any of it."

"He tried to steal from me. He had to be punished." Father's voice remained calm, almost lifeless.

She had to grip her apron to keep from reaching up and shaking him. She'd never wanted to hurt anyone like she wanted to hurt him now.

She couldn't. It would put Gil in far too much danger. She forced her body to stay still, though her breath came in short gasps. "I need a man sent to town." She managed to keep her tone low and controlled. "For more medicines. I'll make a list. And a doctor. Gil needs a real doctor, even if you have to send to Helena for one."

Her father regarded her, his expression emotionless, almost as if she hadn't spoken. It was impossible to read. She'd seen it before, and she hated it.

But she lifted her chin. She wouldn't show how angry she was. "He can't be moved, so the doctor will have to come here.

And we're not leaving tomorrow. We're not leaving until Gil is better."

Her father stood a moment more. Not speaking. Then, with a curt nod, he turned and walked out.

When the curtain swished back into place, she allowed herself to breathe again. Her shoulders sagged, and the rush of air she took in made her lightheaded. She turned to her sleeping area and tied the fabric barrier back again.

Would her father summon a doctor? He guarded their privacy so fiercely, rarely permitting outsiders in.

But surely he would send for the medicines for her *husband*.

Wouldn't he?

Exhaustion pressed so hard on her limbs that she barely dragged herself back to Gil's side. Maybe stitching that gash on his face should wait until he awoke. No sense in ruining precious sleep, though she might have already interrupted his rest with her loud words.

She should probably eat something herself, but her middle churned at the idea. Should she force something down? Maybe in a little while.

First, she needed to have that list ready when Father sent someone for it. She'd run out of paper, though, and had forgotten to pick some up when they were in town last. Would Gil mind if she tore a page from the back of his notebook? She would be careful not to look at anything he'd written.

The book lay on top of his pack, easy to grab and pluck out a single blank page. But when she picked it up, a pencil tucked inside made the cover fall open.

Her breath caught as her gaze fell on the open sheet.

There, sketched in exquisite detail, was her own likeness. She stood by the cookstove, her face turned slightly, captured in a pensive moment. The shading, the lines, the way he'd shown the light falling across her features—it was a work of art, crafted with undeniable talent and a depth of perception that... Well, he was remarkable. His *talent* was remarkable.

Her fingers hovered over the page, not daring to touch the graphite strokes. The drawing let her see herself through Gil's eyes, and the intimacy of it made her throat burn. He had noticed her, studied her, in a way no one ever had before.

She swallowed hard and forced herself to close the notebook, her heart thudding against her ribs. The walls she was working so hard to rebuild around her heart, the ones she needed in order to keep herself safe, were teetering. How could he knock them down so easily, even in sleep?

With shaking hands, she tore a blank page out and tucked his notebook away again. She couldn't afford to dwell on the implications of that sketch, not now. Gil needed her to be strong, to focus on his recovery.

She had to push aside all these tangled emotions, which would overwhelm her if she let them.

CHAPTER 19

*M*iles Coulter ran his fingers along the smooth edge of the metal blade as he stood in Canvas Creek's general store, studying an unusual pickax. The handle had been formed of two parts, with a lever in the middle, which would require less effort to strike and give a harder blow than a man would be able to manage on his own. This tool would surely make cutting into a stone wall a great deal easier, allowing men to get more work done in a single day...or knock off early to spend time with a gal.

Ugh. He'd spent too much time around romance lately, what with all his smitten brothers and their pretty little brides, and young'uns, to boot.

He returned his focus to the tool. It could use a few minor adjustments to optimize its output, but he could easily make those. If he extended the top part of the handle a little longer, it should strengthen the power of each blow. He'd have to be careful not to go too long, though, or the pickax would become unwieldy.

"You've been staring at that thing for an hour." His brother Jude propped a shoulder against a nearby shelf.

"I started drawing it last night, but I can't get the scale right." He needed Gil's talent. His big brother could sketch the thing in perfect details. Of course, if Gil were here, they wouldn't be *here* in the first place. Miles slid a glance to where the clerk was helping a customer. "Do you think they'd mind if I measure it?"

Jude's brows rose. "You could always ask. Or we could just buy it so you can take the thing apart and rebuild it the way you want."

Excitement surged at that idea. "Let's. That's a good idea."

He shifted his focus to the clusters of people milling around the store. "You seen Two Stones yet?" They'd split up from their [Indian tribe] friend that morning, all searching a different direction from town for any sign of Gil or Sampson.

Jude shook his head. "Not yet. But he said he'd meet us here when the sun is three fingers from the horizon." He glanced out the western-facing window. "Which should be about now."

Miles glanced out too, squinting against the late afternoon sunlight. The streets of Canvas Creek were bustling with activity, but there was no sign of their friend's tall, lean frame and pitch-black hair. Had he found someone who knew where Gil had gone? They'd been searching for days now, following every lead and rumor, but he seemed to have vanished without a trace. Just like Sampson had.

A knot twisted in Miles's belly.

A voice sounded from the counter, Mr. Smith asking another customer what he needed. Gil let his gaze wander to the exchange. He and Jude were far enough out of the way that he wouldn't be caught staring.

"Need what's on this list." The fellow slid a scrap of paper across the surface.

Mr. Smith adjusted his spectacles and scanned the note, his balding head gleaming in the late afternoon light slanting through the windows. "Most of these are medicines. Somebody sick?" He turned and reached for bottles on the shelves behind him.

"Just fill it quick as you can. And add a couple bottles of whiskey and a pound of coffee."

As the clerk worked, the customer leaned against the counter, his gaze restlessly roaming the store. When his eyes met Miles's, he looked away.

Was it his imagination or was the man hiding something? Miles left the row of tools and wandered that way, pretending to examine the tins of tobacco lined up near the register.

The stranger drummed his fingers on the countertop. Then he asked, "You got a doctor around these parts?"

Smith paused, a bottle of some dark liquid in his hand. "Nearest one's in Helena, a half day's ride from here."

The man cursed under his breath. "Just my luck."

As the clerk set the last items in the crate beside the customer, the fellow reached for it. "Put it on Mick's tab."

Mick?

Miles straightened, exchanging a sharp glance with Jude as the stranger strode out of the store, the door slamming behind him.

Jude stepped toward Miles and spoke low. "We need to go. Now."

Miles's gaze darting back to the pickax. "Can I just purchase that real quick? Or get one more measurement—"

"Miles." Jude's voice turned urgent. "He's the man Gil and Sampson were searching for. This could be our best chance at finding them."

He turned to follow Jude. "Let's go."

They left the store and turned right, staying a distance behind the man from the store.

In Miles's mind, he called to his brothers. *Hang on, boys. We're coming for you.*

~

Shadows flicked on the rock walls as Jess crept along the corridor, her breath shallow and her pulse racing. Thank God she'd taken the shortcut through the tunnel back from the storage closet, where she'd gathered more willow bark.

The words she'd just overheard echoed in her mind, each one like a dagger to her heart. Her father's cruel instructions to Jedidiah rang in her ears—move the sapphires Gil had found to a new location, somewhere in a different mountain.

Then make sure Gil met with an *accident*.

Nausea rose in her throat.

He would have her husband killed. The father of her child.

Of course, Gil was neither of those things, but Father didn't know that.

If ever she'd hoped she was more important to him than money, the truth was as real as the stone beneath her feet now.

Now that he couldn't marry her or sell her, she was worthless to him.

She slipped into the apartment, doing her best to slow her breathing.

Father and Jedidiah had sounded as if they'd be occupied for a while, so hopefully she and Gil could talk without being overheard.

Now that it'd been a full day since the beating, he was propped up in her bed, his handsome face still mottled with the swelling around his left eye and cheek. Her chest ached every time she looked at him. How much pain must he be in? Especially since he'd refused to take a full dose of laudanum Riggs brought back from town, agreeing to take just enough to take the edge off. He joked about not wanting to sleep all day, but she knew the truth. He needed to be alert, to be ready for the next attack.

Which would come, if Father had his way. And Father always had his way.

Gil's good eye met hers as she approached. Sinking onto the edge of the bed, she swallowed hard against the lump in her throat.

"What's wrong?" He reached for her hand, as he had so many times in the last day. He seemed to crave the connection, as though her touch brought him comfort.

As his touch did her. Being connected to him made her feel stronger. Like she could face whatever lay before them.

She needed that strength now more than ever.

"Gil, I...I just heard my father talking to Jedidiah." Her voice trembled, so she eased out a breath of tension. "He told Jedidiah to move the sapphires you found, to store in another mountain cave."

Gil looked like he was about to ask questions, so she hurried with the rest.

"And then..." A knot clogged the words inside her, and she had to fight the burning in her eyes. "He told Jedidiah to kill you. To make it look like an accident."

Gil's fingers tightened around hers, his only reaction to her words. At last, he released a long stream of air, resting his head back against the pillows that propped him. His good eye focused on the stone ceiling. He must be regretting ever meeting her. *Deeply* regretting that he'd agreed to pretend to be her husband.

"I'm sorry, Gil. I'm so sorry I got you into this mess. I won't let him hurt you. I promise." Panic welled in her chest at all the ways Jedidiah would try. He preferred direct confrontation, with a few of his bullies alongside to make the numbers as uneven as possible. But he could be conniving. And he took delight in torture.

How could her father stand to have that man around?

Except Father was just like Jedidiah. Maybe Jedidiah had learned his ruthlessness from her father.

It didn't matter. Gil had to be her focus now. Him and how she could protect him.

His gaze shifted back to her, his expression frank, as if he'd found the answer. "We have to leave, Jess. Now."

Her insides knotted. "You can't travel. You're injured." And even if they did get out, Jedidiah's men would track them down. "Our only chance of getting free for good is if my father allows it."

His grip on her hand tightened as his one good eye held her gaze.

If she blocked out the other side, it didn't hurt so much to look at him. But even with black eyes and distorted features, this was still Gil, the man who'd committed to keep her and her baby safe. Her free hand already rested on the bump at her middle, and she rubbed her thumb over her dress. *I'll protect you, sweet one. I'll protect you both. Somehow.*

So much was at stake. She couldn't let them make a wrong move.

"I promised I would get you out of here. You and the baby." He shifted his hand to cover the one she'd rested on her belly. The warmth in his eye, the intimacy, the certainty—they nudged the walls she was trying to keep strong.

His voice held steady. "With God as our help, we'll get free from this place. Both of us. *All* of us." The baby too.

She sucked in cool air, letting it fill her chest and lift her shoulders. Letting it clear the panic from her body and the fear from her mind. She'd not included God in her worries or frantic plans. How could she call herself a Christian and have so little faith?

She placed her other hand over Gil's, holding all three of them at her belly. "Can we pray? Now?"

The edges of his good eye crinkled. Then he closed it, and

his rich voice filled the space around them. "Lord. Thank You for being the Good Father, no matter how much our earthly family fails us."

Good Father.

Hot tears seared her eyes. She was only now allowing herself to put into words—if only in her mind—how much her father had failed her. To think of God as Father had always been a struggle for her, though Ezekiel called Him that often. It seemed impossible to think of Someone Who loved her, Who planned good things for her—hope and a future—and also think of Him as a Father.

Gil was still praying, and she was missing his wonderful words, so she tugged her mind back to focus.

"We trust You to guide our steps and protect us. Help us to be wise and discerning as we seek a way out of this situation. Give us courage and strength for whatever we face. In Jesus's name, amen."

She echoed a soft "Amen." The sincerity and steadiness of Gil's words seeped into her soul, fortifying her faith. God was with them. He would make a way, even when there seemed no options.

She opened her eyes to find Gil watching her, a gentle smile on his lips despite the pain that had to be throbbing through his battered face. "We'll figure this out together, Jess. You're not alone anymore. None of us are."

Gil was right, of course.

God had brought this wonderful man to her, a man to show her His love, just as Ezekiel had, yet in a very different way. Her middle warmed as that thought settled.

A very different way from old Ezekiel.

Could Gil see what she was thinking? Why did it seem his smile turned roguish?

She drew in a deep breath, scrambling for a way to refocus

them on the task at hand. "What about your brother? Do you want me to find him and see if he'll go with us?"

Gil's gaze turned distance, pain seeping into his good eye. "He made it clear he won't leave here. I don't want to risk you or the baby to convince him." His throat worked. "Sampson can be stubborn. I guess I have to let him make that choice."

Breath seeped out of her, leaving only the pain that Gil must also be feeling. "I'm sorry."

He gave a grim nod. "Me too."

She inhaled again, mentally searching for the next step. "We need a plan. My father will have guards at every exit, watching for any sign of us trying to leave."

Gil's brow lowered. "We can get to that tunnel that shares the same entrance as this apartment, right? The one that leads to the bunk room? Are there any other passageways I haven't seen? Even tiny ones? Or caves that dead-end?"

She pictured the outside of the mountain in her mind. "I only know of the main entrance from our apartment and the three others—one on each side of the mountain. And they'll all be heavily guarded."

"Hmm." Gil shifted, trying to sit up straighter, though his face twisted in pain.

She adjusted the pillows behind him. His every breath looked agonizing.

When he was settled, he reached for her hand once more, resting their clasp on the blanket. "I think our best chance is to wait until nightfall and sneak out then. Maybe out the front entrance where the grass is highest? I can stand guard with a gun while you crawl low. You can take a gun with you, and once you're clear, you can cover me as I follow."

The image of Gil dragging himself across the ground, each movement pure agony with his battered ribs, made her insides clench. "Are you sure you should do that?" She knew better than to ask whether he *could* do it. Men were stubborn when you questioned their capabilities. At least Father was.

But Gil didn't seem angry. In fact, was that a glimmer of humor in his eye? Surely not.

His fingers tightened around hers, a reassuring squeeze. "I'll manage, Jess. Remember what we prayed, for strength to face what we need to?" His tone held a bit of humor too.

"You also prayed for wisdom and discernment. Those would be wise to use now."

The corners of his mouth tugged upward. "True."

She lifted her hand from Gil's and pressed two fingers to the wound, using the lightest of touches. Maybe she should have bandaged it, but she'd been applying salve every few hours, and the cut didn't fester. If they were on the move, she'd need to protect it from dirt and further damage.

Gil slid his hand around her wrist and pressed a kiss to the center of her palm.

He was such a good man. How could he possibly want anything else to do with her? After they got out of this mess, he would run as far away from her as he could. Maybe he'd make sure she found a place to settle first—his honor might require him to do that much—but then he'd be done with her.

And she'd be alone.

Yet alone and free would be so much better than smothered and miserable, surrounded by all the evil here.

"Jess."

Her name in Gil's husky voice made her heart skip a beat.

She forced a light expression and lifted her brows at him. "Yes?"

He rested their joined hands on his midsection and placed his other on top despite the pain the moment obviously brought, based on how his eyes tightened at the edges. "What are your plans for when you're free?"

No softening the question, just straightforward. As though their thoughts had been following the same trail.

She worked for a casual tone. "I'll find a quiet town somewhere. Maybe in a different territory. Someplace my father and Jedidiah's men won't find me. I'll get work, and we'll have a nice life." Just her and the baby. Free.

His hands tightened around hers. "Would you come back to the ranch with me? To stay?"

Her heart surged. Did he mean…they would…? But no. He'd not offered marriage, just a safe place to live.

As his…mistress? Surely not. Not Gil.

Maybe he meant for her to build a little house on the property like others had. But how would she work? Even if housing weren't a problem, she'd need to buy food. And things for the baby.

"Jess."

Again, the way his voice caressed her name drew her from the churning in her mind.

His gaze was so warm. "I know I only met you a few days ago, but we've been through a few things together." Those lips tugged upward again. "Our situation makes me feel like I know you much better than the short time would usually allow. And one thing I'm certain of is that I want to know you better. I want to court you."

Wait. What? What was he saying?

"I want to know every thought that passes through your mind." His words rumbled deep and tilled hard soil deep inside her. "I want to be there to protect you. And help you. And make sure you never want for anything. Not shelter. Not food. Not all the wonderful things you deserve. And especially not love."

The loose soil lifted as if tossed by a whirlwind.

Did he…? Was he saying he wanted to…?

He lifted her hand to the side of his jaw, the uninjured part near his stitches. "I don't want to rush you. You can take as long as you want to decide. Months. Years. As long as you need. But I want you to know that this is what I've started to dream of. Until you know for sure, though, my family has lots of room for you. My sisters-in-law will fight over who gets to keep you, I'm sure."

Fight? They'd fight?

He pressed a kiss to her fingertips. "In a good way. They'll love you." He must have felt her tension. He lowered their joined hands back to the bed.

Her mind spun so fast she couldn't form words.

He glanced over at his sleeping pallet. "Unless someone's taken it, my rifle should be under my blankets."

Right.

The beautiful picture he'd drawn in her mind couldn't happen until they got out of here.

She had a lot to do to get ready for their escape tonight.

There would be time later to savor Gil's words.

CHAPTER 20

*T*he night air hung thick and still as Gil crept across the main room behind Jess. He worked to quiet his breathing, doing his best to ignore the pain radiating through his battered body, though every step shot pain, which seemed to focus on his ribs.

She paused at the curtain that covered the outer doorway and peered around its edge. He should be the one protecting her, not limping behind.

She stepped back and motioned for him to look through the same crack. The darkness was too thick for him to read her expression, but he leaned in and squinted to see the landscape outside. The moon wasn't bright but cast more light than inside the cave. It only took a second for him to focus.

In the distance, a lone figure stood silhouetted against the inky sky. Jedidiah.

Jess's hand found Gil's in the darkness, and he intertwined their fingers. Her grip held determination and strength.

Protect her, Lord. Her and the baby both. He was still so weak, he wouldn't be nearly enough to keep her safe. Only God could accomplish that feat. Gil couldn't remember a time he'd been so completely reliant on the Father. *Please, Lord.*

Jess gave his hand a squeeze, then pulled away. He inhaled as large a breath as his ribs allowed, then raised his rifle and shifted deeper into the shadows of the opening, where he could see Jedidiah and the path Jess would take.

If Jedidiah saw Jess, would Gil have to shoot him? He'd not hesitate if Jess's life were in danger, but a rifle blast would bring all the guards on the double. He and Jess would have only seconds to run. They'd decided that if someone saw them leaving, they'd sprint toward the creek where their tracks would be covered.

He had to be ready for anything.

Jess adjusted the pack on her back, then dropped parallel to the ground and crawled on her toes and elbows through the tall grass, moving left of the mountain.

As she inched her way forward, Gil couldn't breathe, praying that Jedidiah's keen eyes wouldn't spot her slender form slithering through the underbrush. Each second felt like an eternity as she crept farther from the safety of the cave, farther from him.

Jedidiah hadn't shifted, his dark eyes scanning the night. Did he sense her there, a shadow hiding among the swaying grass?

Gil kept his rifle aimed at the man. If he so much as waved his barrel in Jess's direction, Gil would be ready.

At last, she reached the tree line, about twenty strides away. Relief washed through him.

Now came his turn.

He gathered his strength and lowered to the ground. He lay on his belly as she had, but had to roll to the right so he didn't put weight on his left side, where his ribs screamed in pain. The rocky earth dug into his tender flesh as he crawled, gripping his rifle with one hand. Every movement hurt. He gritted his teeth, forcing himself to keep moving.

Inch by excruciating inch, he dragged himself forward, his eyes fixed on the trees where Jess had disappeared. The tall grass itched his face, and despite the cool autumn air, sweat ran down his brow, the salty drops stinging his eyes as he fought to maintain his focus. Just a little farther. He could make it. He had to.

"Stop!" Jedidiah's bark cut through the night.

Gil whipped his head sideways to see the threat. The man held his rifle aimed directly at Gil.

He froze, his mind racing. He was too far from the trees, too exposed. If he jumped up and ran, he'd never make it before Jedidiah cut him down.

A shot rang out, shattering the stillness.

Gil tensed, waiting for the impact. But Jedidiah's gun hadn't sparked.

He staggered back with a roar, his rifle dropping as he clutched at his shoulder.

Gil struggled to push up to his feet. This was his chance. "Run, Jess!" He shouted the word, his heart screaming for her to get far, far away from this place.

She screamed.

And it didn't sound like she was running. Why?

He finally straightened, one hand gripping his injured ribs while his feet propelled him forward.

He couldn't see her well in the shadows of the trees, but was she struggling against someone? Is that why she hadn't run?

He surged forward, raising his rifle. But before he could take aim, a fist slammed into his jaw, knocking him backward. He stumbled. Pain exploded through his face as he fought to keep his balance. His vision swam.

Through the haze, he made out men emerging from the shadows, their guns trained on him and Jess. They were surrounded, outnumbered.

Finished.

The reality of their situation crashed over him.

They had failed. And the aftermath might prove worse for Jess than anything she'd faced before.

She struggled against the iron grip of the man restraining her, her eyes frantic. "Gil!" Her cry pierced the night, a plea and a prayer all in one.

He tried to move toward her, but rough hands grabbed him, wrenching the rifle from his grasp.

The pain in his ribs flared, stealing his breath.

Lord, please. We need a miracle.

Gunshots cracked the air. How many guards had come running?

The men holding him jerked and spun.

What was this? They seemed surprised, their attention snapping to the new threat.

Through the chaos came a sight he could barely believe. He must be dreaming. Out of his mind from pain. Or maybe unconscious.

Horses galloped into the fray, and were those...Jude and Miles? And Two Stones too.

Hope surged through him. Where had they come from? This had to be a hallucination.

But the bullets whizzing around them were very real. The man holding him jerked, his grip loosening. Gil fought to get his arms free, pushing through the fire in his middle.

The scene unfolded like something out of a dream, surreal and impossible, yet undeniably real. An answer to a desperate prayer.

Two Stones leapt from his horse beside Gil, slamming into the man who still held him. They grappled on the ground, fists flying and grunts filling the air. Gil staggered back, his ribs screaming with each movement, but he couldn't give up now. Not when Jess needed him.

Jude appeared at his side in an instant, hands gripping Gil's arm. "Let's get out of here." He tried to hoist Gil onto his horse, but Gil fought him.

"Jess. We have to get her." He pointed at the trees where she struggled against her captor. Even in the shadows, he could see the way she fought with every ounce of her strength. She must be terrified.

Jude's gaze flicked from Gil to the chaos erupting around them.

Bullets whizzed past, the sharp cracks of gunfire exploding in the night.

"Miles," Jude shouted. "Take Gil and cover me!" He swung onto his horse and plunged his heels into the gelding's side.

Having mounts definitely gave his brothers an advantage.

Miles was already standing beside his mare, firing at the advancing guards. Two Stones had dispatched the man who'd held Gil and now leapt onto his own horse, leaning low and to the side so he wouldn't be a target as he shot toward the guards clustering in the trees.

There were so many of them. No shots came from the direction where Jedidiah had been, though. Either he lay dead or he'd moved around to join his men.

Gil turned back to Jess in time to see Jude had reached her and somehow freed her. He was now pulling her onto his mount.

Thank You, God.

They had to escape.

Jedidiah's men seemed to have multiplied by ten. Even so, somehow, none of their shots had landed—either in horse or human.

Gil moved to his youngest brother and reached up for the saddle. "Let's go!" But his rib made it impossible to pull himself up. The struggle alone lit his body on fire. He collapsed sideways on the saddle, sapped out.

Then Miles pushed him up, and Gil landed in the seat. He

hunched low over the animal's neck, grabbing his ribs to quell the flames inside. The pain seared hot, stealing his focus. He could only make out blurry movements in the black around him.

Miles climbed up behind him, and the horse pivoted, then shot into a run.

The animal's pounding hooves shook every part of Gil, keeping him in that hunched position. One hand pressed hard against his ribs to hold them together, the other clutching the saddle to keep himself aboard.

Jess. He had to make sure Jude got to her. Had the guard harmed her before his brother intervened?

Had she'd been struck or injured badly enough to hurt the baby?

His stomach nearly cast up its accounts right there.

He lifted his head enough to see a horse in front of them. Two riders. Jude in front, and behind him…

A woman with a long braid. *Jess.*

She sat upright, so maybe she wasn't hurt. That was more than Gil could have hoped.

Thank You, God. He let himself slump, honing his focus to staying on the animal and keeping his pain tamped down so he didn't black out.

~

*T*he horses splashed through the creek as Jess gripped the saddle she was seated behind. She couldn't see anything ahead unless she leaned around the bulk of man in front of her, but thick woods lined both sides of the water.

How long had it been since she and Gil crept away from the apartment? Not more than ten minutes surely, or fifteen at the most.

She had no idea who these three strangers were who'd appeared from nowhere on horseback and saved her and Gil.

Guardian angels or kidnappers? She'd never seen them before. They seemed to know Gil, but that offered little comfort. Her father's men were clever and not above deception. Jedidiah might have hired mercenaries from town for this very situation.

The horse she rode stayed in the lead, the rescuer/kidnapper keeping them in the creek bed. Jess had pointed them in this direction so the water could conceal their tracks. But staying in the creek meant they had to move slower to avoid all the hazards in the water.

How long until Jedidiah's men saddled horses and pursued them? Her father only owned six mounts—seven if they used Gil's horse too—and the animals grazed in a valley south of their mountain. It would take the guards a few extra minutes to catch and mount the horses, but then they could move at a faster pace if they stayed on shore, not worrying about leaving tracks.

How much time did they have?

She twisted in the saddle, and her eyes found Gil, slumped over the neck of the horse he rode, just behind her. The younger man sitting behind him met her eyes, but she didn't waste energy on him.

Was Gil alive? Surely, he was. If he'd been shot, wouldn't they be tending the wound or trying to stop the bleeding?

Still, she had to know. "Is he all right?"

Gil raised his head, and relief swept through her. Pain marked his features, and he slumped again, but he was conscious.

"I'm fine, Jess. Are you hurt?" His voice sounded tight and weak.

The question raised the memory of rough hands, the explosion of pain when the guard plunged a solid blow to her jaw.

Because of the angle he'd held her, he'd not been able to use his full force. That probably explained why she didn't have a broken jaw. Yet her head throbbed, the pain shooting through her ear. She would have a bruise there, no doubt.

"I'm fine." She looked to the man riding with Gil. "He has a broken rib. Be careful with him."

The fellow looked barely more than a youth, but dipped his chin. "I've got him." His voice sounded a little like Gil's. Or maybe that was her imagination. Wishful thinking?

She turned forward again, blinking back a sting of tears. The pain and fear and...all of it. It caught up with her. The last hours, her father's cruel decision, Jedidiah's threats, Gil's injuries. Elijah's death.

It was too much. Too much.

She couldn't think about any of that or she'd collapse in a puddle and drip right into the creek.

She focused on the jarring trot of the horse beneath her. The night air. The chirping crickets. The moon that gave just enough light for them to see by.

Each stride took them farther from her father's grasp. And brought them closer to...what? She didn't know.

She *needed* to know who these men were.

She leaned forward so the man in front of her could hear. "Who are you?"

He turned his head enough for his words to reach her. "I'm Jude. Gil's brother." He nodded to the men behind them. "That's Miles with Gil, and Two Stones bringing up the rear."

Gil's brothers.

Relief flooded through her. Not kidnappers or hired guns, but family. *Thank You, God.* He'd heard her desperate pleas and sent rescuers.

"How did you find us?"

Jude guided his horse around a cluster of larger rocks on the right. "We've been looking for Gil and our other brother, Sampson. Trailed someone from town earlier today but lost him." He sounded miffed, and confused. "Guy just disappeared."

Into one of the secret cave entrances, no doubt.

"Anyway, we set up camp near the mountain and heard a gunshot. Got there as fast as we could."

Wow.

These brothers had come for Gil. They'd risked their lives, riding into the fray without hesitation to save one of their own.

Gil would have done that too. These Coulters were unlike anyone she'd ever known.

The creek curved ahead. Soon, they'd reach the place where it split into two streams. She leaned forward again to speak above the splashing water without yelling. "The creek divides up ahead. The right fork winds through a valley. The other flows into a river. I'm not sure if Jedidiah knows about the split. Maybe he does." She couldn't imagine he'd done much exploring, but he knew everything. He likely had maps of the terrain in all directions from their mountain.

"The river will give us more options to lose them," Jude said. "We'll pray God leads them the other way."

Before today, she might have scoffed at such a prayer. How often had she prayed that God would make her father a different man?

After she learned about the baby, she started praying God would help her escape.

Tonight, He'd answered that prayer. In a way so much more remarkable than anything she could have imagined. Now, it seemed truly possible that He would point Jedidiah's men the wrong direction. He really could do anything.

CHAPTER 21

"*Ho.*" Jess forced her eyes open as Gil's brother brought their mount to a halt after a long day's ride. She straightened and blinked to bring into focus a small building in front of them. "What is this?"

"An old trapper's cabin." Jude's voice came low and weary. "Two Stones knew about it. Should be safe for us to rest a while."

She was too exhausted to protest. They'd ridden through the night, staying in the river—in the shallows on the opposite side. Just before dawn, they'd ventured away from the water over a rocky open area, then into the woods.

Not once had they seen Jedidiah's men.

At first, that had been a relief. Yet it felt too good to be true. Was the fight really over?

As the morning passed, she'd dozed against Jude's back. Maybe that had been overly familiar with a man she'd never met before, but he was Gil's brother. He'd saved her life. And anyway, she couldn't have kept herself awake even if she'd wanted to. Perhaps the baby made her more exhausted than she would have been.

Now, she slid from the horse, her legs unsteady as they landed on the ground. She turned to look for Gil. He would need help to dismount. During their travels, she'd given him a couple doses of the laudanum that had somehow stayed in her pack during the fight. Though he took enough to make him sleepy, he'd still be in some pain.

But he'd already made it to the ground, thanks to his brother's help, and now stumbled toward the shack.

She hurried to catch up with him and reached him as he pulled the latchstring to open the cabin door.

A blast of musty air pushed out as the door swung inward. The place looked deserted. Gil stepped inside, and she stayed close to him.

A few log stumps sat around a fireplace on one end. Gil shuffled toward them and lowered to one and sat, squeezing his eyes shut against his pain.

She touched his shoulder. "I'll get blankets and food so you can lie down and eat."

She turned back toward the door, but his voice paused her. "Wait." He nodded toward one of the other logs. "Sit, Jess. My brothers will bring in everything. I'm sure you're exhausted. And the baby…"

Heat flushed up her neck, and she glanced to make sure the others weren't inside yet to hear. "I'm all right. I'll rest when you're settled." Her hand crept up to the roundness at her middle. Could the baby have been injured in the fight? She'd not been struck close to her belly, so surely not.

Had she felt a flutter yet today? Her mind was so numb, she couldn't be certain.

Footsteps at the door pulled her focus as Jude stepped inside, arms full of packs and satchels. "I don't know what all the two of you need. There's food here, though not much. Two Stones is going to hunt so we'll have fresh meat."

She moved to the load. "A bit of food and some blankets will be helpful. Gil needs to eat and rest."

Jude pushed a satchel toward her. "This has food. I'll get the blankets next, then start a fire."

As she opened the clasp and pulled out a leather-wrapped bundle, Gil spoke from where he still sat on the log, his head in his hands. "Jude, if I fall asleep, make sure Jess eats plenty and rests. She's eating for two."

Jess's heart stuttered.

She didn't have the nerve to look at Jude's expression, but he'd stopped walking and was surely staring at her.

Why did Gil tell him? That was her news to share if she chose.

"Will do." Jude's footsteps sounded until they muffled on the dirt outside.

She turned a glare on Gil. He'd lifted his head, not a trace of apology on his face.

He raised a hand before she could speak. "I'm sorry to tell private details like that, but Jude had to know so he can see that you have everything you need." The uninjured side of his face pulled up in a lopsided smile. "His wife, Angela, is expecting too. He'll know how to help."

As much as she wanted to vent her frustration, how could she rail at Gil for wanting to care for her? And the thought that there was another woman in her condition at the ranch where they were headed... If she already had one thing in common with one of the inhabitants, maybe she wouldn't feel like such an outsider.

The leather bundle held strips of smoked meat—the same as what Jude had shared with them on the trail. The aroma made her stomach twist and release a hungry gurgle. She handed two pieces to Gil and bit into her own. She'd not realized how very hungry she was.

When Jude returned with a load of rolled blankets, she laid out one while he spread the other. Then she helped Gil shift to his hands and knees, then lower onto his back.

He released a long slow breath, his eyes closing. "That's better." Then he lifted one lid to look at her. "You should lie down too. It feels awfully good."

"He's right." Jude had moved to the fireplace and knelt to gather the burnt scraps of wood. "There's nothing else to do. Miles is feeding the horses, and Two Stones already caught our dinner. He's skinning it now."

She lowered herself onto the blanket she'd placed beside Gil's. Was it improper to lie so close to him now that they weren't pretending to be married? His brothers and friend had asked very few questions, but they had to be curious.

Probably, this would be the time they'd want answers.

As Jude built a fire, Gil's fingers found hers, his rough palm sliding against her own. The simple touch felt so intimate, maybe because they were both lying down. Yet she couldn't make herself pull away. The warmth of him, the solid strength in his grip, felt like an anchor in the chaos.

The flames seeped warmth into her bones and chased away the chill that had settled deep within her. She'd had Jude's solid form to shield her from most of the wind as they'd traveled up and down mountains, but the weather seemed much colder in these parts than around their cave home.

Miles and Two Stones entered together, the younger Coulter brother rubbing his hands against the cold. Two Stones carried something to the fire. She couldn't see what he was doing, but that must be the dinner he'd caught.

She'd always purchased their food in Canvas Creek, so she'd rarely eaten fresh game and had only seen it cooked once. One of the miners had been broiling a hare in the bunkhouse last year when she was there stitching a cut closed on another fellow's face.

Gil squeezed her hand, and his good eye opened to look at her. She must have tensed with the memory.

She forced her hand to loosen. He tightened his grip though. "What's wrong?"

A rush of tears sprang to her eyes, but she forced them back. When would she stop being assaulted by emotion at the most inconvenient moments? She worked for a serene tone. "Nothing's wrong."

He stroked the back of her hand with his thumb. Gentle. Patient. "You don't have to pretend, Jess." He kept his voice quiet enough that its low rumble probably didn't reach the others. "Not with me."

To not have to pretend—to be strong, to be unmoved by the horror of the world.

Once more the tears surged, and she sniffed to hold them back. "I was thinking about the only other time I've seen wild game cooked over an open fire. I was stitching a gash on a man who'd been beaten by Jedidiah's guards." She glanced up at his face, letting herself take in the awful bruising. The wound she'd stitched on him just yesterday. "His injuries weren't nearly as bad as yours."

That one corner of his mouth tipped up again. Surely it hurt him to move even that part of his face. Yet it was the only sign that showed he was trying to smile. "Mine aren't so bad. At least I have an excuse to keep you close."

She couldn't hide her own smile, but thankfully, the dim cabin hid the way her cheeks must have turned pink. "You don't have to get beat up for that."

She'd meant it in a teasing way. But in truth, the idea of leaving Gil's side made her heart race. Staying with Gil meant safety.

Was that the only reason she wanted to cling to Gil? Safety?

If she didn't have to worry about her father or Jedidiah finding her—if she could travel anywhere in the world—would she still want to stay near the Coulter Ranch, close to Gil? She did need to worry about them though. Her father would send someone after her. Surely. He'd done it before.

But even if her safety weren't in question, she couldn't imagine leaving Gil. She couldn't imagine a life that didn't include him. She couldn't imagine ever feeling complete apart from him. He'd become her safe haven, yes. But he'd also become...a friend.

Miles settled on one of the log stumps. "You two up for answering a few questions?"

Could she summon the energy? She'd have to.

At least Gil's grip on her hand stayed solid as he spoke. "Sure. Figured you all were curious."

Miles's expression took on the hint of a grin. "What happened out there? We got worried when we came back to Canvas Creek to help you look for Sampson and couldn't find you."

"It's a long story." Gil shifted to better face his brother. "I was searching farther out from town. One day, I found Jess on the mountain. We started talking, and I realized that her living situation wasn't safe. She needed help getting away from her father. Simon McPharland. Most people call him Mick."

Tension seeped into the air, so heavy it could smother. Apparently, his brothers knew that name well.

"Jess is nothing like her father though." When Gil spoke again, his voice popped the bubble like a pin. "Not a single bit. She's tried to escape him before, but his men found her and brought her back. One in particular is a lousy son of scum. Jedidiah, McPharland's second in command."

He cleared his throat. "We figured the only way to get her free with her father's approval was to pretend to be married.

The ruse worked pretty well for a while. We were nearly set to leave. I even got to talk to Sampson a few times too."

Jude's head snapped up. "You found him? Where?"

Tension rose once again. "He's working for McPharland. In the mine there in that mountain where you found us."

Jude's brows lowered. "Why? Doesn't he know what kind of man McPharland is?"

"I think he knows." Gil's voice roughened. "He says he's not finished there yet. Wouldn't come back with us."

Miles leaned forward. "Did you tell him we've been looking for him? That we're all worried?"

"Yeah." Gil blew out a breath. "I begged him to leave with us. To come home or go somewhere else. Any place not under McPharland's thumb. He refused."

The silence stretched, broken only by the crackle of the fire. "So," Jude finally said, his words slow and deliberate. "What do we do now? Go back for him?"

Gil's fingers tightened around Jess's. "I don't think that's wise. At least not yet. Jess needs to get to safety first. To the ranch."

Jude seemed to be mulling through the situation. "You're probably right. We might need the others so we can go back with more gunpower."

Gil shifted on the blanket, a wince tightening his features. "There's something else. We found some of the sapphires."

Jude straightened on his log. "You did? Where are they?"

"McPharland had them hidden in one of the storage caves. I think it's only about half of what was stolen. Jedidiah caught me trying to get away with them. Probably moved them after that."

Miles scowled. "Is that how your face got rearranged?"

Gil gave a soft chuckle that looked more like a grimace. "It's not as bad as it looks."

Her chest ached with those words. She had no doubt he hurt every bit as much as the bruising and swelling made it seem.

"Anything else?" Jude looked between the two of them.

"That's about it." Gil sounded weary.

Jude turned his focus on her, and her chest tightened as she prepared for what he might say. He knew more of her father's awful deeds now. Would he throw her out? Take her back to face her punishment?

Gil would speak up for her. Wouldn't he? Anything seemed possible. The very worst seemed possible.

But Jude's eyes softened. "I'm glad Gil found you. Glad we were able to get you out. You get some rest now." He glanced over at Two Stones, who still sat by the roasting meat. "What do you think, should we head out about midnight?"

The dark haired man nodded. "Best to ride when we won't meet others." Two Stones had been mostly quiet until now, but his voice held a rich tone. His words were clear, almost without accent, though he didn't use many to make his point.

Jude nodded, then shifted back to her. "We're near the Mullan Road, and that's a straight shot back to our ranch. But it gets a fair amount of travel that we'd rather avoid."

"Good thinking." Gil's words slurred a bit as his eye closed.

"All right then. Sleep for now. Food should be ready when you wake up." Jude pushed to his feet and moved to the pile of packs.

She let her eyes drift shut.

She should release Gil's hand so he could rest better. Settle into her own space on the blanket and sleep.

But she couldn't make herself let go of him. Not now, and maybe not ever.

CHAPTER 22

The next day, the sun hung low in the western sky, casting the woods they traveled through in shadows. Jude had said they were nearing the ranch.

The steeper terrain kept Jess clinging to his coat to hold on, fighting the exhaustion that pressed constantly. The gentle rocking of the horse had lulled her into a doze several times in the night and this morning, her head resting on Jude's back. But she never let herself fully surrender to sleep. She couldn't risk tumbling from the saddle.

Their trail opened into a clearing, where she spied a sturdy barn directly ahead and a house up the hill. Jude loosed a piercing whistle, and moments later, the front door swung open.

A woman stood on the stoop, studying them for a moment. It didn't take her long to recognize the men, for she hurried down the steps, and four other women followed close behind. A young girl skipped along with the group.

As they approached the horses, it was easy to see the moment each of them made out the disfiguring bruises and swelling on Gil's face. All approached Gil and Miles first, except one dark-haired woman who went straight to Jude.

His wife, no doubt. Angela.

Jude bent down from the saddle to press a quick kiss to her lips. Jess looked away to give them privacy, but not before she caught the utter joy on Angela's face to see her husband again. How long had the men been gone?

Jude straightened and motioned to Jess. "This is Jess McPharland. She rescued Gil and brought him back to us. Jess, this is my wife, Angela." He pointed to the other women gathered around Gil. "And this is Dinah, Naomi, Patsy, and my niece Lillian. The little one in Naomi's arms is Mary Ellen, and that young lady next to her is Anna."

Angela sent a welcoming smile. "Don't worry about remembering names. There are a lot of us. It's a pleasure to meet you, Jess." She reached up a hand, and Jess placed hers in it. Was that what she'd wanted her to do?

Angela's smile warmed, and she squeezed Jess's fingers. "I'm so glad you've come. Let's get you inside. You must be hungry and exhausted."

Angela helped Jess dismount, then guided her toward the house with a gentle hand on her back. Her touch felt almost motherly. Hadn't Gil said Angela was expecting too? She slid a glance to the woman's middle. Her dress was full enough that it was impossible to discern a sign of her condition.

Should Jess have expanded her dresses to conceal her growing waist? She'd not thought to. She could now, though, if one of these women would allow her the use of needle and thread.

A pang pressed in her chest. She didn't even have her own sewing supplies. She needed to start earning money soon so she could buy the things she'd left behind.

That worry could wait until morning, at least.

Lillian trailed them while the other women assisted Gil. He'd said his oldest brother's wife, Dinah, was a doctor. That must be her, the woman with the lightest blond hair, judging by the way she took charge of Gil's care.

As they entered the log cabin, the warmth and bustle of the others enveloped her. The women moved about with purpose, their chatter filling the air—a far cry from the solitude she was accustomed to, but there was a comfort in their presence, a sense of belonging that Jess had never experienced before, not even before her mother died.

She stayed in the main room while the women settled Gil in one of the bed chambers, the one Patsy had been occupying, apparently. The red-haired woman gathered her belongings and slipped out with them, then climbed a ladder attached to the wall up to a loft.

None of the men entered the house except Gil, and through one of the windows, she could see Jude and Two Stones lead their horses into the barn. Was Miles already inside the building with his mount?

"Let's get food for you both." Angela's voice sounded behind her, and Jess turned to see her and the young woman, Lillian, working together near the cookstove.

As she watched them work, she gripped her hands together. She was usually the one doing the work. But she didn't want to force her help on them—or her presence in their kitchen.

Angela glanced up, her dark eyes meeting Jess's with warmth. "Why don't you have a seat at the table? You must be exhausted."

Jess slowly lowered herself onto one of the wooden chairs around the long oval table. The ache in her muscles eased as she settled. Lillian set a steaming mug of tea in front of her, the delicate floral scent wafting up to her nose.

"Thank you." She wrapped her hands around the warm cup, letting its heat ease her tension.

Angela brought over a bowl of steaming soup. "I'm sure you're famished after your journey."

"Thank you." Two such small words, but what else could she say?

Angela settled in the chair next to her. "Jude says you rescued Gil?"

Heat flushed her cheeks, and she shook her head. "More like he rescued me. He helped me get away from my father." She searched for another way to explain without having to tell the entire story. Gil would likely share everything, but that felt like such a long conversation, and she couldn't find the energy to start it yet.

Angela rested a hand on the table. "It sounds like you've had a hard go of it. I'm sorry."

Jess took a bite of stew as she searched for an answer. Something other than *thank you*. Or a false reassurance like *It wasn't so hard*.

Angela spoke again though, saving her the trouble. "I haven't ever had to escape my father, but I remember when I first met Jude. We were traveling west on a train, then we moved to a steamship. At one point, we realized we were being followed by men I'd worked with. It turned into quite an ordeal, and at one point, I wasn't sure Jude or I would make it out alive." Her gaze had turned distant, but now she refocused on Jess, shifting her hand to rest on Jess's arm. Her warm tone nudged aside some of the distance between them, making Angela feel more like a friend. "I'm glad you had Gil. He's a good man. I'm sure the two of you were a great help to each other."

Jess could only nod and take another bite. She needed this food more than she'd realized.

The front door opened, and a man stepped inside. She'd not seen him before, but he looked a little like an older version of Jude.

Jude followed him inside, trailed by Miles, Two Stones, and

another man. A third stranger brought up the rear, closing the door behind him. His auburn curls looked as different from most of the others as Two Stones's rich black braids did.

The first man—probably Jericho, the eldest, if she had to guess—aimed straight for the open door to the room where Gil lay. But Jude scanned the room until his eyes caught on Angela's. He moved toward her like a magnet, stopping behind her chair with his hands on his shoulders as he bent to press a kiss to her cheek.

Once again, Jess tried to look away quickly enough to give them privacy, but she couldn't help but see the way Jude's hand dropped to his wife's middle for a second, before pulling back.

Jess focused on her food and gulped down another bite.

"How are you both and our sweet babies? These ladies know how to make a stew, don't they, Jess?" His eyes twinkled as he spoke. He didn't seem embarrassed about mentioning their unborn babe in front of her, as though the child already wiggled on the floor between them. As though he was happy about their coming gift.

Blasted tears burned her eyes again, and she willed them away so neither of these nice people saw her emotion. If only she'd done things differently. If only she'd not wanted control so desperately that she'd pushed Alex so far.

She might one day have a husband who looked at her the way Jude looked at Angela. A husband who wanted children with her, offspring of their love.

If only she could go hide away with Gil. Sit by his bed without all these strangers around. She was safe with him. And she didn't have to wish things were different.

With Gil, she didn't have to try to be what he wanted. She only had to be. He accepted her exactly the way she was.

Nay, he did far more than accept her. He looked at her almost the way Jude looked at Angela. Not exactly the same. Gil possessed a bit more charm and flair than this brother. Something she loved about him. A trait that had drawn her from the very beginning.

Jude and Angela were looking at her now, as though waiting for her to speak. Had they asked her a question? She searched the recent conversation in her mind. Jude had asked how she liked the stew, then...

He dipped his head closer to his wife's ear, drawing attention from trying to remember what she was supposed to answer. When he spoke, his words were quieter, meant for Angela, but he sent a smile to Jess.

"Miss McPharland is expecting a little one too. Like us. I told her you'd love to talk to her. Maybe she's experienced that heartburn you've been struggling with."

Angela's eyes widened, yet not in horror. Pleasure bloomed over her face, and she took Jess's hand in both of hers. "Oh, Jess. How wonderful."

Jess worked for a smile. Angela had surely realized that Jude called her *Miss*, not *Mrs*. Most women would shun her, from what she'd gathered from the doctor and a few books she'd read.

But Angela didn't stop with squeezing her hand, she moved her arms to Jess's shoulders and pulled her in for a hug. "Jess, I'm so, so very glad you've come. I know we just met, but I feel like we've been friends for years. There's something about you that makes you seem like a sister."

Jess stayed still for a moment, not daring to move lest she do something wrong. She hadn't been hugged by a woman since... since Mama. And that had been twelve years before.

As Angela squeezed, Jess returned the embrace, which felt like the right thing to do. She settled her hands on Angela's back and let herself breathe in the hug. Angela smelled like stew and roses, a combination so real, her body gradually came to life.

Maybe for the first time since they crept away from the only home she'd ever known in the middle of the night.

Tears welled, burning so fiercely she couldn't hold them back. As they leaked down her cheeks and into Angela's hair, a sob forced its way up her throat. She couldn't cry on this woman. This stranger.

Yet she couldn't stop herself. With Angela's soft arms around her, her body chose to break through the numbness that had been holding her together the last two days.

Oh, God. This hurts so much.

She wasn't even sure where all the pain came from. Leaving her home, her father. Seeing the awful things Jedidiah's men did to Gil. Knowing she was part of the reason that had happened. Knowing her father was the man behind it all. Knowing her father was such an awful man, yet still wanting him to love her, to call her his daughter and look at her with those eyes that said she'd done well. That he was pleased with her.

And Mama. If only Mama were still alive, these past eight years wouldn't have been so hard. Yet would they really have been better? She would have been able to share the weight of her father's actions—and the weight of what he wanted for her —instead of bearing it alone. She could have shared the weight of his expectations, which she'd felt compelled to fulfill, no matter what.

But could she really wish her mother had been there to endure all that? How could she be so selfish? Such a selfish daughter.

The more her mind spun, the more sobs heaved out of her, tears long since blurring her eyes so she could see only outlines of the cabin around them.

She had to pull herself together. She could apologize for this outburst and somehow move on from it.

Maybe Jude and Angela were the only ones who'd seen her collapse. Perhaps they wouldn't tell the others.

When she finally reined in the emotion and pulled back from Angela, the poor woman's hair and shoulder were completely soaked. Jess sniffed and wiped one eye, then Angela pressed a cloth in her hands. "Here."

Jess used it to wipe the other eye and her nose, then sucked in a long breath as she took in Angela and Jude.

A hand pressed her shoulder from behind, and she spun to see who was there.

Gil sat in the chair beside her.

Her heart leapt, and a fresh wave of emotion clogged her throat. Gil.

That one good eye twinkled at her, its warmth the home she'd been craving. Part of her wanted to curl into his chest and let him hold her. She couldn't do that of course. Not with him injured and here in front of his family.

Speaking of his family, if Gil had come in here, where were the others? The women and the men who'd come in with Jude?

A glance around showed that the door to the room where Gil had been lying was closed. Were they all in there? Surely not. They must have gone outside. To get away from her crying?

Heat flushed her ears once more, but Gil's warm hand slipped under hers, weaving their fingers together. Calling her back to him.

"Anything I can do?" His voice was low, almost intimate.

He hadn't asked what was wrong. Gil seemed to always know what she needed. He probably understood why she'd been crying more than she did. And he'd left his bed—injured as he was—and come out here to be with her.

He stroked the back of her hand with his thumb, a gesture that already felt so familiar, and she shook her head. "I'm all right. Truly. I think it just all caught up to me."

"I know what you mean." He nodded past her. "I see you've met Angela. She's one of the good one's. Not quite as bossy as Dinah."

Angela pressed her lips in a smile. "Don't listen to him. Dinah's wonderful. Like a mother hen to us all."

A grin tugged at Jess's cheeks, despite everything. She needed to try to explain what she was feeling to Angela. "I've never really been around women. My mother died when I was eight, and then it was just my father and me. The only people around us were men who worked for us. My only friends were the miners, though I didn't know them well."

She ducked her chin a little. "I've never really been around women. Not like this. In a group. I've…wanted this, but…"

Angela chuckled. "We're a little overwhelming, I know exactly what you mean." She glanced back at her husband, who'd taken the chair behind her sometime during Jess's crying fit. "Before Dinah and Naomi came, it was just the six brothers and Lillian and Sean. Poor Lilly had to put up with all those boys."

Angela's smile lit her eyes as she gripped her husband's hand. "We've been adding to the ranch, one by one. Mostly wives so far, but soon we'll be adding more little ones." Her other hand clasped Jess's fingers. "We're so very happy you came, Jess. I hope you'll stay a long, long time."

A new round of emotion rose in Jess's throat, but she forced a smile to clear it away. She had to change the subject before she started crying again.

She turned to Gil. "Did you eat? This stew is wonderful."

His mouth curved. "I did and it is. Almost as good as yours." Then he squeezed her hand. "Come on. I told Jericho we'd give the whole story soon, and I don't think I can hold him off much longer."

She rose from her chair along with the others and braced herself for the coming conversation. The Coulters would be angry at her father. Some of them might even see her as the enemy. But Gil would be at her side through it all.

And maybe Angela and Jude too.

As the family gathered and pulled chairs into a large circle in front of the hearth, Gil led her to a bench with a back and armrests that was wide enough for two. He settled in beside her, still not releasing her hand.

Angela took the chair on Jess's other side, with Jude next to her. Murmurs filled the room while others settled into the remaining seats.

As she took in the group surrounding them, something inside her eased.

A family. All these people were Gil's family, and so far, they seemed kind and willing to accept her. Even when she'd shown such weakness.

Gil's thumb stroked her hand again, and she turned to him. That good eye soaked her in, it's warmth undeniable.

"I'm glad you're here." He spoke quietly, his words only for her.

She swallowed down a fresh lump in her throat. "I am too."

And she truly was.

CHAPTER 23

"Can I walk with you back to Jude's? I'm going that way."

Jess slid a glance at Gil as they strode up the slope from the barn to the main house. "You happen to be going that way?" She couldn't help teasing. Only rocks and trees lay in the direction of Jude and Angela's cabin.

He gave a casual shrug. "I'm going that way if you are." The corners of his mouth tugged. "I told Jude I'd bring him a bag of nails too."

With the warm afternoon sun chasing away the deepest autumn chill and almost a full day spent with Gil and the Coulter women, how could Jess not smile?

These five days since they'd arrived on the ranch had been a little slice of heaven. A heaven she'd dreamed of but hadn't been sure even existed this side of eternity.

The only thing that spoiled her peace was the ever-present threat of an attack from her father's men. Gil's brothers were keeping guard, though, and not one of them treated her like she was connected with her father's sins in any way. She'd never expected to feel so welcome here. Or anywhere, for that matter.

She hadn't experienced a similar feeling since her mother's passing.

Watching Gil interact with his family gave her so much insight into how he'd come by his easy charm. The tender affection in his smile as he played with his nieces, the little girls' delighted giggles ringing out across the yard. The respect and camaraderie evident in his conversations with his brothers.

And when his gaze met hers across the room, the warmth and tenderness there stole her breath. She could imagine a future where she belonged on this ranch. With Gil. Where her child would be surrounded by love and laughter. They would both be free from the shadows of her past.

"Is that a yes then?" Gil nudged her back to the present with his words.

She sent another look, this time maybe a little coy. "I suppose that would be fine."

They both knew she wanted him near anytime he could manage it. His ribs were starting to heal, and since Dinah wrapped them in a tight bandage, he'd been out of bed far more than he'd rested. The swelling had almost completely left his face too. Now when he smiled—as he was doing at the moment—both sides of his mouth rose equally.

The bruises had lightened to a pale yellow-green. An awful color, truth be told, but at least she could better see the real Gil through the bruising.

They reached the house, and he opened the door for her.

"Let me just get my heavier coat and I'll be ready." She stepped inside and pulled her jacket from the peg by the door.

Dinah emerged from her bed chamber, wiping her hands on her apron. "Heading back down the mountain?" Her smile felt so warm and genuine. Like a motherly elder sister.

"Yes, Gil's walking with me." She couldn't help the hint of pleasure that crept into her voice. It'd been wonderful having him so near these past few days.

She'd been staying with Jude and Angela, which was about a ten-minute walk from the main house, close enough she saw him and the others often. But it was nice to have the quiet there with Angela too. Neither Angela nor Jude talked overmuch, which was a relief. And for the first time since Jess had learned of the baby, she could finally speak openly about her condition and ask Angela all the things she'd wondered.

With a final wave to Dinah, she and Gil stepped back into the crisp mountain air.

As they walked the worn path to Jude and Angela's cabin, Jess breathed deeply, savoring the sweet scent of pine and wood smoke that always seemed to hang in the air here. Peace settled over her, a peace she'd only ever found in Gil's presence. With him, the burdens of her past seemed to lift away. She could be open with him, free to speak her thoughts.

He'd already witnessed her greatest shame—her father's evil —and he didn't blame her for it. He treated her like she was her own person, not permanently soiled by her blood connection to Simon McPharland.

Gil showed her so much respect, far more than she deserved. Sometimes so much she didn't always know what to do with it.

They walked in companionable silence for a time, arms brushing occasionally.

The babe delivered a firm kick on her right side, and she pressed a hand there, rubbing the spot. If only she could rub the tiny foot instead, cradling little toes and kissing them.

Gil's gaze slipped into her awareness, and she glanced over to see him watching her with uncertain eyes. "Is everything all right?"

"All is well. The little one kicked harder than usual."

Something flickered in his warm brown eyes. Longing? Curiosity? He didn't speak at first, but the air grew thick between them. Her stomach twisted. Was he wondering about…?

Finally, he cleared his throat. "Jess, I know it's not my place to ask, and you don't have to say if it's too hard, but..." He tucked his hands in his coat pockets. "The baby's father. Who is he?"

She'd known this question would come eventually, but a part of her had hoped to avoid it forever. Shame heated her cheeks as she remembered her foolish choices with Alex.

Gil deserved the truth, no matter how much it pained her to speak it.

If he grew angry and sent her away, better now than before she became too comfortable here with his family. But even as that thought slipped in, she pushed it back. Gil wouldn't send her away.

He would be disappointed, though, and she hated the thought of him looking at her like that.

Yet he *should* be disappointed in her. She was disappointed in herself.

She slowed to a stop. They would reach Angela's cabin soon, and she didn't want this conversation overheard.

She took a breath for courage but could only fix her gaze on a branch ahead of her. "His name was Alex. He worked for my father. I thought..." She shook her head. How could she put into words what she'd done? What she'd been thinking. "I let him go too far. I...I encouraged it even. I thought it would give me power, a way to take back control of my life." She could barely breathe through the weight on her chest.

Did she need to say more?

She risked a glance at Gil's face, bracing herself for the disappointment, and probably even judgment, she was sure she would find there.

But those eyes she loved didn't hold censure, only a deep sadness that echoed the ache in her heart. "Jess. I'm so sorry."

The grief in his tone made the knot in her middle twist even tighter. The last thing she wanted was to bring him more pain. He should be angry at her, not share in her pain.

His mouth parted like he wanted to say something, so she waited. He searched her face as he spoke. "What did you do when you found out...about the baby?"

She swallowed hard. "I started to suspect after a couple months. When I was fairly certain, I snuck away to Helena. I saw a doctor there who confirmed it." Her voice caught, so she took a breath before continuing. "Then I started asking around about Alex. But Jedidiah and his men found me before I could go any further."

His expression turned sober. "Did he hurt you? Or did Jedidiah?"

She shook her head. "No."

Gil took in an audible breath, his shoulders rising as he blew it out. This didn't feel like an interrogation, despite how he watched her. Maybe because he kept his voice so low and gentle.

"Did you love him? Alex, I mean." Though his tone didn't change, she felt the tension in his words.

She turned to meet his gaze. "I never loved Alex. What I allowed with him was a foolish decision, one I've wished I could take back so many times. One I've begged God to forgive me for." She had to swallow down the sting of tears.

She lifted her hand to the swell of her belly, a touch that was becoming so natural. So automatic. "I'm thankful for this babe, though. I know now that God wouldn't have allowed him or her to grow unless He had a plan. And I get to be part of that plan. I'm praying every day that He'll help me raise this babe to be a godly man or woman."

As Gil studied her, the corners of his eyes creased. Not quite a smile. It was more like he was thinking hard on what she'd said. Slowly, he reached out and rested his hand on her arm, the warmth of his touch seeping through her coat sleeve. Then he slid his hand down to cover hers where it rested on the curve of her belly. His larger hand completely enveloped her own.

He looked up to her eyes and locked his gaze with hers. "Jess, I'm so sorry you've had such a hard life. I'm sorry you didn't have a father who could show you what real love looks and feels like. But I need you to know—God forgave you the very first time you asked. He doesn't hold your past against you."

Emotion welled in her throat. She knew the truth of Gil's words in her head—Ezekiel had told her that—but hearing Gil say them with such conviction made them sink deeper into her heart.

He moved his hands to her elbows and tugged her closer, sliding his arms around her back, cradling her in the security of his embrace. "I've known from the very beginning that God brought us together for a reason. And Jess." His eyes searched hers. "When you're ready, I want to take the next step with you."

The next step? Did he mean...?

"I'm not rushing you at all. I know you need time. I just want you to know where I stand, so you don't have to worry about the future...or make other plans."

Her heart quickened, hope and longing swirling together. Even now that he knew the truth, he wanted her?

Keeping one arm around her, he took her hand in his free one. Once again, he pressed her palm to her belly and covered it with his own. "I want to help you raise this little one. I want to be a father to him or her, to show a reflection of God's love, as close as I can get. I want to love you and our family—whatever that family looks like—for as long as I live."

Tears blurred her vision. This man—this wonderful, honorable man—wanted her, broken past and all. Wanted to build a life with her, wanted to be a father to her child. It was more than she'd ever dared hope for.

"You don't have to answer right now." His words came quick, as if he saw the overwhelming emotion on her face. "Take as long as you need to heal, to decide when you're ready. I'll be here always. I promise."

He pulled her close.

She snuggled in, laying her head on his chest, one hand resting over his beating heart.

Peace and contentment, more complete than she'd ever known, eased through her. Cocooned in Gil's embrace with her unborn child sheltered between them, the trials of her past finally felt far behind her.

This was her new beginning. No, *their* new beginning.

She tilted her head back to meet Gil's tender gaze and smiled through her tears. "I want that too."

He rubbed moisture from her cheek with his thumb, then lowered his head to brush the sweetest of kisses across her lips.

This man.

With Gil by her side and God's grace to guide them, surely they could weather any storm and build a life—a family—grounded in faith and love. Together.

And she couldn't wait.

~

I pray you loved Gil and Jess's story!

Miles finally gets his story in the next book in the series, and what a surprise he's in for as the danger to his family's ranch escalates...

Turn the page for a sneak peek of *Guarding the Mountain Man's Secret*, the next book in the Brothers of Sapphire Ranch series!

Did you enjoy Gil and Jess's story? I hope so!
Would you take a quick minute to leave a review where you purchased the book?
It doesn't have to be long. Just a sentence or two telling what you liked about the story!

To receive a free book and get updates when new Misty M. Beller books release, go to https://mistymbeller.com/freebook

ALSO BY MISTY M. BELLER

Brothers of Sapphire Ranch

Healing the Mountain Man's Heart

Marrying the Mountain Man's Best Friend

Protecting the Mountain Man's Treasure

Earning the Mountain Man's Trust

Winning the Mountain Man's Love

Pretending to be the Mountain Man's Wife

Guarding the Mountain Man's Secret

Saving the Mountain Man's Legacy

Sisters of the Rockies

Rocky Mountain Rendezvous

Rocky Mountain Promise

Rocky Mountain Journey

The Mountain Series

The Lady and the Mountain Man

The Lady and the Mountain Doctor

The Lady and the Mountain Fire

The Lady and the Mountain Promise

The Lady and the Mountain Call

This Treacherous Journey

This Wilderness Journey

This Freedom Journey (novella)

This Courageous Journey

This Homeward Journey

This Daring Journey

This Healing Journey

Call of the Rockies

Freedom in the Mountain Wind

Hope in the Mountain River

Light in the Mountain Sky

Courage in the Mountain Wilderness

Faith in the Mountain Valley

Honor in the Mountain Refuge

Peace in the Mountain Haven

Grace on the Mountain Trail

Calm in the Mountain Storm

Joy on the Mountain Peak

Brides of Laurent

A Warrior's Heart

A Healer's Promise

A Daughter's Courage

Hearts of Montana

Hope's Highest Mountain

Love's Mountain Quest

Faith's Mountain Home

Honor's Mountain Promise

Texas Rancher Trilogy

The Rancher Takes a Cook

The Ranger Takes a Bride

The Rancher Takes a Cowgirl

Wyoming Mountain Tales

A Pony Express Romance

A Rocky Mountain Romance

A Sweetwater River Romance

A Mountain Christmas Romance

9 781954 810952